Reflections of Yellow Brick

Roxas James

[i]

-To You

Reflections of Yellow Brick

Prologue

Kansas - 1908

Gray. The whole world looked gray. The clouds blanketing the sky banished all the color from the surrounding area. The small house had once been a healthy shade of brown. That was when it was new, but after many brutal summers, the wood had been beaten until it looked as bland and dreary as everything else. The overwhelming plainness of the harsh Kansas farmland made it all seem so grim.

Dorothy Gale was too lost in her daydreams to think much about the dreariness of her home. In her mind, she could only see blue skies and green grass. Uncle Henry said she spent too much time in her own head and not enough in the real world. Auntie Em had a few other comments on the matter, none of which Dorothy liked very much. But what neither of them could realize was that Dorothy's mind could not stay in the "real world", not after all that she had seen.

It had been several years since Dorothy even mentioned the land that she had visited. When she first returned from her fantastical adventure, she could talk of nothing else. Auntie Em hadn't the patience for such flights of fancy, but Uncle Henry enjoyed the stories about witches, wizards, and munchkins. But his tolerance could only be expected to last for so long. He was the farmer of land that was not always the most fertile. His mind had to be firmly planted on the ground.

But after what she had been through, Dorothy could not just let those memories go. No matter what her guardians told her about her over active imagination, she would never say it wasn't real. The extremes that she had to endure would make normal girls crack under the pressure. Dorothy was stronger than that, the kind of strong that came from knowing she was right. Not even the hospital in Topeka broke her. All it taught her was to keep quiet.

And that's what she did. Not a single word came from her mouth about Oz or its people. That seemed to please her aunt and uncle. Their niece was cured of all her delusions and was fit to take her place on the farm. And not a moment too soon. Ever since the twister that caused all the trouble to begin with, the farm had been in serious danger. The workers had to be let go. The bank was constantly knocking on their door for payments that they couldn't afford. The Gale farm needed every member of the family pulling their weight.

It was all an act though. Dorothy knew what her family

wanted and that's what she gave them. Her mind was a different story though. Quietly, she relived memories in her head that her aunt and uncle could not touch, no matter how much they might want to. For a long time, she hated them because of what they did to her, but she couldn't keep that up for long. They just didn't understand. But how could they? They hadn't been there and seen all the wonders she had. It wasn't their fault their minds were stuck in dreary old Kansas. And in those hidden memories she remembered that no matter how beautiful the land, she spent most of her time there trying to find a way home.

Hidden underneath the chicken coop behind the barn, Dorothy kept a battered old book of blank paper. It had taken her months to save up enough money to buy it from the little store in town. In was even harder keeping Auntie Em from finding out about it. If she did, it would be right back to the hospital for Dorothy. It's not that her aunt would disapprove of the book itself, but the colorful pictures that filled most of the pages were another story. The entire book was crammed with as many pictures as Dorothy could fit inside. Squat little Munchkin houses. Yellow bricks looping through green fields. Towers of the Emerald City reaching towards a blue sky. Not even Uncle Henry would be amused by her drawings.

"Where is that lazy girl?"

Auntie Em's voice jolted Dorothy out of her daydreams. She had been so consumed by her drawing of the Wicked Witch of the West's castle that she hadn't heard anyone moving around the side of the barn. As quickly as she could, she threw the book underneath the coop and covered it with the stray straw that somehow found its way to every inch of the farm. She had just enough time to make a basket out of her skirt and scoop a couple eggs into it before her aunt stepped around the corner.

"There you are, Dorothy. You're uncle has been looking for you." She had a stern look on her face and a weathered basket hanging in the crook of her arm.

"Good morning, Auntie Em." Dorothy hid the tremor in her voice well. It had taken years of practice, but worth it if it kept suspicions off her.

The harsh look melted from her aunt's face when she saw the eggs collected in Dorothy's skirt. Clearly surprised, it took a second before she held out the basket so the eggs could be put inside. "Thank you, Dorothy. I was just coming to do this. How long have you been out here?"

"I came out here early this morning. It was a little too hot in my room last night, so I didn't sleep very well. I woke up long before you and Uncle Henry, so I came out to the barn to get an

[4]

early start on the day's chores."

Knowing that her work would be checked meticulously, Dorothy made sure to feed and brush the horses before settling down with her book. She was sure that her aunt would not be able to find any fault with her work, no matter how the old woman tried. If Dorothy was going to sneak away to indulge herself, she had to make sure not to give her guardians any reason to suspect her. She had to play her part.

"It's a good thing you did. Looks like there's a storm coming."

Both sets of eyes turned to the sky. Dark gray clouds rolled through the air. Dorothy thought they looked angry, like they were mad at the land and about to take their rage out on all of them. She didn't say this though. Auntie Em would not be happy. Pretending that objects acted like humans was something her aunt would never tolerate, even before. "It looks like a bad one."

"That it does. The weather has been pretty clear the past couple months. We're due a big storm." Auntie Em picked the last of the eggs from Dorothy's skirt and placed them in the basket on her arm. "Give me those. I'll take them inside. You go out to the field and help your uncle tend to the cows. He's having a hell of a time with Elmira."

[5]

"He's always having a hard time with that cow. He really should sell her. Or turn her into a nice dinner for us." Dorothy hated that cow and had ever since it tried to sit on her when she was milking her. She swore the big, dumb animal had done it on purpose.

"Don't let Uncle Henry hear you say that. You know she's his favorite." Their laughter sounded strange in the air, mainly because it wasn't heard very often. Dorothy could count on one hand the number of times she heard her aunt laugh out loud. And she never thought it would be because of that stupid cow.

With the last egg deposited in the basket, she started to walk towards the field where her uncle would be waiting. Before she could get far though, Auntie Em grabbed her hand and pulled her back. Dorothy was wrapped tightly in the old woman's arms, but wasn't sure if she should return the hug. If laughing was a rarity coming from Emmaline Gale, hugging was downright unheard of. The one and only time that she could ever remember getting an embrace like that was when she arrived home from her trip to Oz. Finally, she put her arms around her aunt and squeezed back.

"Thank you, Dorothy."

When they moved apart, there was a strange look in Auntie Em's eyes. It was hard to tell the reason for it because that look had never been seen on the old woman's face before.

Sometimes, Dorothy felt like the farm was no place for emotions.

Her aunt's hand ran across the girl's cheek, the callused fingers scratching against smooth skin. "I love you, child."

Dorothy knew there were times, especially in the last couple of years, that her aunt and uncle regretted taking her in after her parents were killed in that boat accident. It was hard not to know that. The pained looks on their faces spoke louder than their words ever could. But they did take her in and had never tried to send her away for good. That, more than anything, was the reason Dorothy couldn't hate them for dismissing Oz.

"I love you too, Auntie Em. I always have."

And just like that, the moment passed. "Now get on, girl. Your uncle will never get that cow moving on his own."

Dorothy walked away from the chicken coops and around the barn, but she felt like skipping through the fields. She couldn't remember the last time she had done that. Her aunt would say that a girl her age didn't have any place skipping. And true, Dorothy was now pushing towards eighteen years old, but she had never felt her age. The only reason she stopped in the first place was because she couldn't stand to see the looks of disappointment that it caused.

[7]

Just as she was about to throw caution to the wind and skip out to meet her uncle in the pasture, a wet nose slammed into her leg. Sometimes the dog had to resort to such measures to get her attention. "Good morning, Toto." She picked the scruffy dog up and cradled him in her arms. From her skirt pocket, she pulled out a small meat scrap that she had been able to save from dinner the night before and fed it to him.

Toto wasn't as young as he used to be. Before, a morning like this would have been spent chasing chickens or barking at pigs. But recently, all he had been able to muster was a few weak yips from the front porch. Occasionally, he'd take a slow walk through the fields, but usually only at Dorothy's side.

Throughout the years, the dog was the only one she could talk to honestly. Even though he couldn't say so, she knew Toto remembered that distant land and everything that had happened there. If Dorothy had to keep her memories hidden from her family, at least she could have conversations with her dog about them. And with an imagination like hers, sometimes it felt like Toto could actually talk back.

The dog looked up at the sky and let out the weakest of barks, causing Dorothy to follow his gaze. The gray clouds had become even darker and angrier. They were moving much faster than before. The storm would be on them in minutes. If she didn't hurry, her uncle would never get all the animals under shelter in time. And knowing her guardians as well as she did, they would still be working in the middle of a downpour.

Dorothy quickened her pace, covering the distance between her and her uncle as quickly as possible. When she got to the pasture, Uncle Henry had somehow convinced that obstinate, old cow into the barn and was busy herding the rest of the cattle to cover.

"Dorothy, child, run and fetch Goldenbrick! He got spooked and took off behind the tool shed!"

That stallion was, by far, the most cowardly animal Dorothy had ever met, and that was saying something. At the slightest breeze, the horse would lose his nerve and hide. But Dorothy couldn't help but feel an affectionate bond with him. Goldenbrick was the first horse born on the farm after she came back from Oz. It was so soon after that Auntie Em didn't even object to her naming him after the fantastic land.

Dorothy placed her dog on the ground so that she would be able to get the horse. There was no way that she would be able to control the stallion and hang on to her lifelong little friend at the same time. It didn't bother Toto any. He was content to follow at Dorothy's heels, his natural place in the world. In truth, he could do without going to see that Goldenbrick though. The two were not the best of friends, for reasons that had nothing to do with being different species.

It wasn't until Dorothy turned the corner of the tool shed that she noticed how strong the wind had become. Intense gusts blew at her dress and hair, threatening to take her off her feet. The quick and drastic change told Dorothy just how powerful this storm would be. There was sure to be damage to the farm. That wouldn't help Uncle Henry's mood any and make more work for the family. Despite growing up on a farm, working it harder wasn't something that Dorothy was looking forward to.

She found Goldenbrick right where her uncle said, hiding behind the tool shed. Carefully, she inched closer. "Easy, boy. It's just a storm." Dorothy reached out to pet the horse's mane, but he jerked away from her hand. His black eyes showed a fear in them that the girl had never seen, even in all the storms that had hit over the years. He bumped into the dry wood of the tool shed, as if the little building would protect him.

Dorothy tried to touch Goldenbrick again but was met with the same failure. If she didn't calm the horse soon, he would most likely start to buck and do serious damage, perhaps to Dorothy herself. She had seen that behavior in in the other horses, but never in Goldenbrick, whose calm nature always struck her uncle as unnatural.

Toto chose that moment to give a bark and not a small,

weak one that had been his latest custom. It was the bark of a much younger dog, demanding and insistent. That was the only way to be heard because the wind had gotten so loud that it drowned out most other noises.

Dorothy, for the first time she could remember, ignored the dog. Her focus needed to be on the horse. Maybe if she had spared a small amount of her attention, she would have been able to hear the faint shouts from her aunt and uncle. But she didn't, and because of that, things went from bad to worse very quickly.

With one hand holding her hair down to keep it from blowing in her face, she used the other hand to reach out for a third attempt at Goldenbrick. The horse consented to the small act of being touched. Under her fingertips, Dorothy could feel just how badly the horse was shaking. It felt almost like some of that fear traveled between the two of them through her hand. Goldenbrick appeared to lock his dark eyes on Dorothy's blue ones. And, in what seemed like a strange time for her imagination to be running wild on her, she swore she heard the horse shout, "Run!"

But she didn't have time to find out if it had been real or some strange trick of her mind. Toto, tired of being ignored, decided to take the most efficient route to getting her attention and bit her on the ankle. It was only a small nip, but more than enough to accomplish his goal.

Just as Dorothy spun around to admonish the dog, she saw it. Clear across the farm, near where the back border fence stood, the clouds were starting to spin, forming a spiral that reached towards the ground like a giant hand. To her, it looked like someone had pulled a drain in the sky and all the anger she had seen in the clouds was funneling towards the earth, like a sink. As she stood, hypnotized by the sight, the vortex of wind grabbed for the ground. When it slammed down, a massive dust cloud erupted into the air, taking a big portion of the border fence along with it.

The tornado had arrived. And with it came change, just like it had done seven years before.

"Oz." Her voice was barely above a whisper, not that anyone could have heard it anyway. The cyclone's landing had been accompanied by a crashing boom that cancelled all other sounds. Dorothy had no hope of hearing her own voice, much less the frantic shouts coming from the other side of the tool shed. She couldn't even hear Toto's insistent barking at her feet.

The tornado was the only thing present for Dorothy. It struck her how things had changed. The last time she saw one, it filled her with a dread that sank all the way to her bones. But that's not what filled her when she looked at the violent twister.

She was consumed with the beauty within the destructive force, along with the secret that it was not simply a tornado that had come to destroy her farm. It was a summons.

Without being conscious of her actions, Dorothy took a step towards the cyclone. All thoughts of Toto and Goldenbrick were erased from her mind. All there was for her was the tornado and getting to it. After all these years, Oz was calling her back. There was trouble, and she was needed. There was no choice but for her to answer that call.

And that's what she intended to do. Her feet picked up speed, taking her to the twister that was moving quickly towards her and the farm.

Uncle Henry was just coming around the corner of the shed to find out why Dorothy hadn't returned without that stupid horse. Inwardly, he cursed the girl's sense. Why wouldn't she just leave the beast and save herself? Then they could be in the storm cellar with Emmaline, safe. He resolved to sit that girl down for a serious talk when the storm had passed.

He saw Dorothy running, not away from the storm, but towards it. "What is she thinking?"

In Henry Gale's day, he could run laps around the farm, but as he got older his legs couldn't keep up the same pace that once drove his daddy crazy. But watching his niece running to her death was inspiration enough for him to call upon untapped reserves of energy and sprint after her. He didn't know how his knees were not giving out, and he didn't ask questions, only used it to close the gap between him and Dorothy.

When the big, rough hands grabbed Dorothy's shoulders, she did her best to shake them off. She tried to be like one of the horses when it was spooked, but the hands remained firm. The grip was determined with no hope of her breaking it. Strong farmer's arms followed and Dorothy's progress towards the tornado was halted.

"Are you insane, girl? You'll get yourself killed?"

"Let me go!" Dorothy screamed into the wind. Her voice strained to levels that it had never reached before. "They need me!"

If Uncle Henry heard his niece over the howl of the storm, he showed no sign. Despite her flailing, he began to drag Dorothy away from the tornado and her certain death.

"You don't understand! They're calling for me!" She managed to get one arm free of her uncle's grasp, but it didn't do much good. He just strengthened his hold, wrapping his arm tightly around her waist. She reached out for the cyclone, as if she could bring herself to it just by force of will.

Uncle Henry didn't have time to give much thought to the girl's strange behavior. He only cared about getting clear of the storm's path, so he could find his wife and get them all to the cellar. And despite the fact that he was able to drag Dorothy past the tool shed, he was not able to increase the distance between them and the tornado. But it wasn't much further to the storm cellar.

'If this blasted girl would just stop fighting,' he thought angrily.

Henry loved his niece, had since the day she was born. If he didn't, he would never have fought so hard to convince Emmaline to take her in when his little sister and her husband had died. He had been heartbroken when he found out the couple had been killed while traveling on the Mississippi River. But having their daughter on the farm kept them alive in his heart. He had never questioned that decision, not even during Dorothy's "problems". But the tornado had clearly snapped something in her head.

No matter how hard Dorothy struggled, she could not break her uncle's grasp. Slowly, he was pulling her further away from where she desperately wanted to go. She couldn't make him understand that it wasn't just a tornado out there. It was because he didn't believe in Oz. His closed mind immediately threw out the idea. But Dorothy knew the truth. She couldn't let her uncle keep her from it.

The door to the storm cellar lay open flat on the ground. It was lucky for Henry because there was no way he could let the girl loose long enough to open the hatch. Emmaline must have had the good sense to do it before heading off to search for Dorothy herself. With the cyclone so very close, they should have already been barricaded inside.

With all the kicking and screaming, Henry was left with no other choice but to throw the hysterical girl down the cellar steps. She would be right mad, but it had to be done. Emmaline was still out there and had no idea that Dorothy had been found. With all the strength he could find in his old body, he launched the girl down, watching her tumble into the darkness below. His best hope was for her to be hurt just enough that she wouldn't be able to climb back out while he searched for his wife.

He was granted his wish because Dorothy hit her head on the hard packed dirt and was immediately knocked out.

***

It could have been minutes. It could have been days. Dorothy had no sense of time when she finally woke up. Her head pounded so fiercely that it hurt to open her eyes. Pain assaulted her as she tested her body. She didn't believe that

[16]

anything was broken. She was able to move; it just hurt to do so.

Carefully, she got to her feet and fought the urge to throw up. It took her a second to realize where she was. She had no memory of how she had gotten down into the cellar. What was the last thing she remembered? Images flooded her mind like an attacker. Goldenbrick. The tornado. Uncle Henry. Where was he? And Auntie Em?

It took painful steps, but she slowly made her way up the creaky wooden stairs that would lead her aboveground. The door was easy to push open, mainly because several wooden slats were missing from it.

Outside, her eyes were attacked by color. For a second, she thought that the twister had accomplished its mission and taken her back to Oz. The sky was a vibrant blue that could rarely be found in Kansas. White puffy clouds lazily made their way overhead. She allowed herself a small smile for being back after so long.

Then she saw the barn standing exactly where it should, but with a missing roof. The chicken coop was fallen on its side, a couple of chickens dumbly poking around it. Pieces of the fence that Dorothy herself had helped put up were strewn across the ground. A massive pile of wood and glass was laying heaped on the ground in front of her.

It wasn't Oz. She was still on the Gale farm, only a twisted version of it. Looking at the destruction wrought by the storm, she knew that the pile of rubble was all that remained of her family's house. There was not a part of the farm that had been spared.

Tears sprang into Dorothy's eyes as she took it all in. What had the tornado done? But it was a call from Oz. They needed her there. Why would they send something to get her that would destroy everything? It made no sense. Would they have known what calling her would cause?

Dorothy made her feet move, taking one step and then another. She wanted to run, but there wasn't enough power in her aching body. Opening her mouth to call to her aunt and uncle, her voice failed her. The only thing that came out was a raspy croak that no one would have been able to hear, even if they were standing right next to her.

As she slowly made her way through the damage, she felt the urge to vomit more and more. Everything she saw was destroyed in some way. Nothing was left whole. How could the cyclone have done this? It looked like it followed a path that would lead to every last building on the farm. How many years would it take to repair it all?

She stumbled as her foot caught on a plank of wood

that used to be part of her bedroom wall. The weathered pink flower that Dorothy had painstakingly painted looked strange amid the rubble. Even though her body wanted to stop, fall to the ground, and pass out, she could not stop moving through the farm. Each new ruined item broke her heart even more. That was until she came upon the spot where the front porch previously stood.

Then her heart completely shattered.

The patched up porch roof that had managed to be saved from the old house was on the ground in pieces. The broken bodies of her aunt and uncle clutched each other underneath the debris. Even as they were facing their death, they still managed to hold on to each other for one last moment together. Dorothy began to tremble where she stood.

Blood stained the dirt around the bodies, giving it a grotesque look. Dorothy hit her knees without even caring what was soaking into her dress. Her hand reached out to touch the faces of the two people who had spent ten years caring for her. Her fingers stopped just before touching a spot of dirt on Auntie Em's face, blocked by some invisible force.

Pulling back, she changed course. Her eyes flashed with anger as she began attacking the rubble covering her aunt and uncle. She had to get them free. They could still be saved. It

[19]

could not end that way, not with everything her family had given up for Dorothy. They could not just be gone.

She lifted a sheet of wood that was suffering from years of rotting, chunks of it crumbling in her hands. It didn't matter that the wood felt spongy and gross, she'd rip it all to shreds if she could, if it meant her family would be free. Finally, in frustration, Dorothy grasped as hard as she could and launched it the air.

The sound of its crash back to earth didn't register in Dorothy's ears. The entire world of sound was replaced with her heart pounding in her ears. Underneath that board was the shaggy, brown body of Toto, his legs sticking out and tongue hanging limply from his mouth. If it weren't for the unnatural twist of his neck, she could almost convince herself that the dog was just taking a nap. All the fight left her body at the sight.

Next to Toto sat Dorothy's book. Was it blown there by the wind or had the dog gone to fetch it, saving it from the tornado? Would he have understood how important that book was to her? There was no way to know.

The book lay open, it's stiff, brown cover in the dirt. A picture faced the sky. It was one that Dorothy had worked hard on, spent many days trying to get right. It showed a golden brick road moving off like a ribbon across the land until it reached a city on the horizon. The spires of the Emerald City reaching all the way to the clouds. It had taken hours to get just right.

Oz. She couldn't help her own family, much less help Oz.

A scream came from Dorothy's mouth. A scream so loud and long that it sounded like it came from a frightening other world. The sound echoed over the ruined farm and into the sky. It seemed to stretch on forever, threatening to never end.

But it did end. And when all the pain and anger and hate had been temporarily released from her body, Dorothy fell to the ground, unconscious, oblivious to the devastation that surrounded her.

Chapter 1

Oxford – 1871

Nineteen year old Alice Liddell woke with a start, sitting up in her bed. Searching the dark room, she could not find anything that would have jolted her from such a deep sleep. What had it been? Had a dream startled her so badly that she was awoken so violently? Alice believed so. She could still hear the echo of a scream ringing in her ears. Had that been the part of the dream that had disturbed her sleep?

She got out of bed, making sure not to step on the pile of books that she had so carelessly left strewn on the floor before going to bed the night before. With only the moonlight streaming through the small part in the curtains to guide her footsteps, it was not an easy task. Her mother would be very cross in the morning when she discovered the mess in her room. Not to mention the lecture she would receive about wasting so much time reading fanciful stories. She had heard her mother's speech so often that she had it memorized. And, yet, it never changed anything.

Making her way across the room, she found the stash of

matches hidden in her drawer. It took her a moment to orient herself enough to strike a match and light the oil lamp on top of her dresser. The small flame pushed back the darkness, bringing Alice's room into focus. As her eyes adjusted, she searched for anything that could have made a noise loud enough to wake her. But the only thing was the collection of stuffed white rabbits with their strange eyes that seemed to follow her around the room. They made her skin crawl, but her mother refused to allow her to dispose of them, all because they were gifts from that ridiculous Mr. Dodgson. All the more reason they belonged in the rubbish.

Turning her back on the vile rabbits, she moved to sit on the side of her bed. It wasn't until then that she realized her heart was racing. Whatever woke her had given her quite a fright. She placed her hand on her chest and felt the mad thumping underneath her white nightgown. Touching her head with her other hand, it came away damp from her sweat.

"Maybe it was only a fever dream," she said, her voice awkward in the silent room.

But it did not feel that way, not to Alice. She couldn't remember details, it was just a feeling in the pit of her stomach. Whatever it was that had invaded her sleep had been real. It might have been hidden. Or simply invisible. Or from another land.

Alice stopped herself before more thoughts of other worlds came to her. It had been almost a decade since she had allowed herself to have such thoughts. Ever since she had returned from her trip to Wonderland and had to endure countless angry rants from her parents about childish flights of fancy, that part of her had been locked away. Sure, she would lose herself in a book or two, but never would she think of the possibility that the worlds inside of the books were real. She didn't need a repeat of what happened last time.

It was all that Mr. Dodgson's fault and his writing of that ridiculous book. He took all her adventures that she spent hours and hours telling him and completely bastardized them. He turned them into ludicrous dribble. And he took all the credit, telling the world that they were merely tales he used to tell her and her sisters while rowing on the river. What's worse is that people congratulated him on a great feat of literature.

He was a fraud and a truly reprehensible man.

When Alice tried to tell her family the truth of the matter, they dismissed her. At first, it was gentle reprimands and insistence that whatever she thought she experienced was simply a dream brought on by the book. She tried repeatedly to get her parents to understand, but they would hear none of it. They lost their patience many times, threatening to send her away to live with a family friend in America if she didn't come to her senses. Even her sisters had stopped listening to Alice's protestations.

It was only a matter of time before Alice had to stop thinking about her Wonderland adventures altogether. She would never deny that they happened because they did. And they were nothing like what the rude Mr. Dodgson wrote. But ever since then, they had been her stories and hers alone.

The only benefit to the whole episode was that she had been able to distance herself from Mr. Dodgson without her parents questioning it. She believed they were secretly glad for the rift. Though they forced her to keep the gifts he sometimes sent, peace offerings for the transgressions that only they knew about.

Alice climbed back in the bed and pulled her blanket up to cover her legs. She knew she should have snuffed out the lamp, but she did not want to be in the dark just then. Her father would most likely reprimand her for wasting oil. It seemed like all either of her parents did was lecture. But she wasn't going to stop her reading in the middle of the night, no matter how much they complained. And she would use as much oil as necessary to banish whatever haunted her room that night.

[25]

Shadows flickered across her walls. Her eyes followed them, seeing images that weren't really there. One thing her parents told her that happened to be true was that her imagination was much higher than ordinary. They said it could get her in trouble one day. To Alice, being able to see things that other people too often overlooked didn't seem like such a bad thing.

A shiver ran through her body. She didn't necessarily feel cold, but she wrapped her arms around herself nonetheless. Something was in the room with her. She didn't have to be able to see it to know that it was there, hiding in the darkness somewhere. It was watching her. A feeling told her that eyes were looking, not just at her, but through her. She pulled the blanket up higher, somehow trying to block the invisible stare.

Alice wanted to believe that it was just her imagination, but she knew better. She had far too much experience with that troublesome cat going invisible on her to question that something unseen lurked in her room. The trouble was Alice had no idea how to fight something that she could not see. Without the use of her eyes, she didn't even have a way to know if this unseen entity meant her harm.

Was it possibly a creature from Wonderland, perhaps the Cat himself, was coming back after all this time? Were they

[26]

wanting her back in that curious land? Perhaps the Queen of Hearts was making a nuisance of herself again and Alice was needed to set her right. Or something new.

She had to confess that the thought of returning did not much appeal to her. Unlike what Mr. Dodgson would have the world believe, Wonderland was not a place of childish fancy. Parts of her adventures she remembered fondly, like chasing the White Rabbit or flying with Gryphon. But other parts, she wished to forget, like Hatter throwing tea and calling her all sorts of nasty, cruel names, or her fight with the Queen of Hearts. To anyone who read "That Book", Alice might sound a little crazy. But in the real Wonderland, the Queen had turned out to be merely a nine year old girl who had let her power go to her head. So many things were different in the real Wonderland.

Another chill rocked her body, but not from some unseen force. She had actually felt it. A whisper of a breeze had passed down her arm. Not strong enough to have come from some creature, but enough to chill her to the bone. It was all the proof she needed to be certain that she was not alone in her room.

Her eyes scanned the room quickly, but thoroughly. Nothing. To her eyes, she was alone with the strange rabbits

[27]

and the antique mirror that stood in the corner closest to the window. It had been in that same mirror that she caught her first sight of the White Rabbit before falling into its depths. In all the years since, the looking glass had stood there, perfectly ordinary. Many times, Alice would let her fingertips slide across the smooth surface and been met with only solid glass.

But huddled under her blanket, the mirror looked different. She couldn't quite place in what way it did, but there was a strange quality to it. She looked intently at the glass, trying to picture exactly what was off. Then it came to her. Somehow, the reflection did not quite line up with the room. There was a small, but distinct variance between the world and its mirror image.

As she scooted out of her bed, the heavy blanket dropping to the floor, she felt the strange breeze again, only stronger. But since she had a visible target to inspect, she didn't give the trick of the wind much thought. Her bare feet padded softly across the room until she stood in front of the mirror.

What she saw did not surprise her. Her reflection looked identical to Alice in every way, right down to the loose fitting cotton nightgown. Alice honestly didn't know what she expected to see. It was a mirror after all. Its purpose was to show you yourself. But hers was no ordinary mirror. Everyone else might just see a regular looking glass, but Alice knew what

[28]

secrets it was capable of keeping.

She was just turning to go back to her bed when the unexpected did happen. As she spun on the ball of her foot, her mirror image did not do the same. The other Alice just stared back at her serenely. The right hand of the image reached up and curled around the elbow of her left arm, something Alice had repeatedly done as a child. A small half smile formed on the mirror Alice's face.

Alice was rooted to the spot in front of the mirror. She could not think of what to do. Should she reach out and try touching the glass again? Would she be met with a different result from all the times before? Would the solid glass give way under her fingers and ripple like it had done all those years ago?

Before Alice could decide on anything, the reflection tilted its head. "They need you, Alice. You must help them."

"Who needs..." Her words were cut off by a strand of her dark hair slapping her in the face. It wasn't until then that she noticed the ghostly breeze had increased in strength. It had become a full blown wind, right there in her tiny bedroom. The pile of stuffed rabbits tumbled from their perch and scattered on the floor.

"I don't..." Again her words were cut off. As the wind had gotten stronger, the noise level had grown louder too. She could barely hear her own voice over the howling. Surely, someone in the house would hear and come to check on her. Such a strange aberration of weather could not go unnoticed, not when it occurred in a bedroom on the second floor with the window closed.

Her nightgown whipped against her bare legs. Alice was left no choice but to hold her hair tightly to her head so she could continue to see. In the mirror, however, her reflection stood perfectly still, smiling, showing no signs of being caught in the wind storm.

"Come." The word came from the mirror itself with an eerie echo that had no trouble being heard over the roaring wind.

Before Alice's eyes, the glass in the mirror began to ripple as if it were water that just had a pebble thrown into it. The image of the mirror Alice distorted into the waves. When they settled again, the image was completely different and all together quite impossible. No longer did it reflect the room that it stood in. Instead, Alice could see a gray sky stretched over what looked like a farm that had seen better days. On the horizon stood a towering funnel that stretched from the clouds all the way to the ground. Alice had learned about such phenomenon in her studies of the natural world, but had never seen one in person.

The tornado was moving quickly across the land, throwing up a thick cloud of dust into the air. It was leaving a trail of destruction in its wake. Alice stood glued to the spot, watching as the tornado moved closer and closer to her. As it did, it began to fill the mirror's surface until it was the only thing that could be seen.

The wind in her room had grown even stronger. Alice was having a difficult time keeping her feet to the carpet. Her whole body swayed in the draft. Why had her mother and father not come to her room to check on her? They must have heard the racket coming from within the room. Was something keeping them from coming? Had something happened to them?

A particularly strong gust knocked her forward. She barely had enough time to grab the mirror frame before her face smashed right into the glass. But no matter how much she pushed back, Alice was unable to right herself again. The wind had gotten so strong, almost as if it were pushing her towards the mirror.

Finally, her body did not have enough strength to hold on. The wind swept her feet from under her. Her hand made the first contact with the mirror. But instead of the solid glass she was expecting, she felt the familiar sensation of it giving way like a peculiarly dense liquid. And then she was gone, falling into a rippling pool that had once been a looking glass.

A ghost of her scream echoed faintly in the furious wind.

Chapter 2

It was the jarring impact on hard ground that brought Alice back to herself. She had the faint recollection of spinning in what she could only assume was the center of the tornado. The ride was surprisingly gentle considering the fury of the wind that had surrounded her. Judging from the various bits of debris that she saw flying around in the swirling storm, she had it fairly easy.

The whole time she rode the storm, she was struck by the impossibility of the situation. She had seen her fair share of impossible things, but being sucked into a mirror by a violent tornado was far beyond the point of reason. Was it possible that she was still in bed and was suffering from delusions brought on by a very high fever?

What else could explain the tornado? Alice had traveled through the looking glass before to journey to Wonderland and it hadn't involved being harshly pulled from her room in middle of the night. Even by Alice's very loose definition, that was not normal.

Though she was not moving at nearly the speeds one

would expect from being caught in such winds, hitting the ground came as quite a shock. Being so consumed by the sights around her, she didn't even notice the earth rapidly approaching. The impact was too much for her bare feet to take and they crumpled, causing her to crash most unladylike to the ground. Her nightgown had given up all pretense of modesty, hitching itself around her upper thighs, presenting a sight that would make her mother frown.

It was only then that Alice had the presence of mind to take in her surroundings. She had come a long way from her quiet bedroom. Before her was a vast expanse of horror. It looked like something that might come straight from a child's nightmare. The sky was filled with a strange darkness, like a more menacing version of nighttime. Green and purple tinted clouds looked as if they were boiling over her head. Alice could not recall ever having seen such an odd sight before.

But the land around her was just as horrifying as the sky. There appeared to be no life left anywhere. Not a single blade of grass sprang from the barren dirt. It looked to Alice like someone had come along and scooped it all up, leaving behind only the waste.

In fact, the only thing she could see besides dirt was a . dilapidated house, though not the kind she was used to seeing. It was crooked, leaning on a corner lodged into the dry dirt.

Several wooden planks were missing from the structure and the roof was all but gone. Clearly, it had seen better days, but still Alice could tell that it had never been a beauty.

"Dorothy, you've changed."

The voice shocked Alice more than anything else she had experienced that night. Jumping to her feet, she spun to see where it had come from. Unnoticed before that moment, stood two people that Alice did not recognize. That in itself was not exactly strange considering she didn't recognize anything around her. One was a woman with dark blond hair pulled back and hanging over her shoulders. She had a pretty face, one that had obviously been more beautiful at one point, but had since seen some kind of hardship. She wore a dress of the palest blue material that clashed with the harshness of her surroundings.

The other person, the one who had spoken, was a man. Or the approximation of a man. Something was off about him, like whoever had created him didn't quite finish the job. Alice stared, despite knowing it was rude to do so, but she couldn't help herself. The man's body was weirdly lumpy. She had no way of making out his face because he wore some sort of mask that was painted to loosely resemble a face. Underneath his crookedly placed hat, Alice could see strange strands, like straw, sticking out.

[35]

'How bizarre,' she thought.

The woman stepped closer to Alice, much closer than she was comfortable with, but she made no effort to move. She felt that if she did, it might offend the woman. That didn't strike Alice as a wise move, since her intentions were still unclear. She helplessly stared into the woman's eyes, which happened to be the exact same shade as her dress.

"This is not Dorothy." Her voice was soft. It immediately put Alice at ease. How could a person with such a soft, calming voice have ill intentions? "What is your name, child?"

It took her a second to find her own words. "Alice. My name is Alice Liddell, ma'am."

The woman's eyes went slightly out of focus for a moment before focusing again. "Alice. That's such a pretty name."

When the woman did not continue talking, Alice decided to take the next step. "Pardon me, for I don't mean to be rude, but who are you? And where am I?"

The woman's face broke into a smile, one that Alice could tell did not come easily. It had an unnatural look compared with the troubled look in her eyes. "I'm sorry, dear, it is us who are being rude. You were not who we expected. My name is Glinda. My friend is called Scarecrow." The lumpy man gave a small bow at the mention of his name. "As for where you are, this is the once beautiful land of Oz."

"Oz? I've never heard of such a place before."

"That is not a surprise, Alice. You come from the Other Land. Very few people there have ever heard of it."

For a second, Alice tried to imagine that she had never been to Wonderland before. She would probably have had a harder time believing what she heard. But since she had had her own experiences with other worlds, it was easier to accept that yet another place existed.

"I thought I was being taken back to Wonderland."

Glinda gave a small laugh. "I'm afraid I've never heard of it. I'm not familiar with many places in the Other Land. Is that where you come from?"

"No, ma'am. I'm from England. Oxford to be more precise. Wonderland is a place I visited before. I'm not sure that it's part of this Other Land, as you call it."

"How strange? Do you happen to know…"

Glinda's words were brought to an abrupt halt by Scarecrow stepping forward and putting his oddly shaped hand on her shoulder. "I hate to interrupt, but we have to leave." His peculiar, unreal eyes were peering off into the distance.

Both Glinda and Alice turned to follow his gaze. Quite unnoticed, another tornado had formed in the vast expanse of dirt. It was still some distance away, but it was moving with impressive speed. Strangely enough to Alice, it did not make nearly the racket as the one that had previously appeared in the mirror. Her eyes were transfixed to the sight.

"Scarecrow is quite right. It is no longer safe here." Alice couldn't help but notice the change in Glinda's voice. It had lost its soothing quality. There were definite traces of panic in it.

Hands were on Alice's back, not pushing roughly, but also making it clear she had no choice as to where to go. The three were moved away from the twister, but it was gaining on them quickly. It only then occurred to her, as she ran through the dirt, that she was barefoot. If only she had known she was going, she might have thought ahead. But can one ever prepare for such a journey?

As they ran, Alice chanced a look behind them. Guided by her new companions, she had no trouble keeping her feet moving, which worked for the best since her attention remained glued to the raging tornado. Before her eyes, it changed direction, away from them. Its new course would lead it straight to the dilapidated house. There'd be no saving it, not in the condition it was in.

Sure enough, seconds later the cyclone slammed into the house with a force that Alice had never witnessed before. The impact was so great that she felt it even though she was a good distance away. Her heart beat faster as she watched chunks of wood being thrown in the air.

Alice turned, her eyes wide. Her feet began to run faster, desperate to get away.

"I'm definitely not in Oxford anymore."

Chapter 3

Alice's feet were killing her. The three of them had been walking for what felt like hours. She couldn't be certain because the sky gave no clues. Neither sun nor moon hung in the sky, so she had no way to tell what time of day it was. The only thing she could see was the blanket of roiling clouds over her head. It felt like she was under a fierce darkness with no end.

Her two new friends attempted to make the time pass with the only tool they had available to them, conversation. Question followed question from the time they were safely clear of the massive tornado. They wanted to know everything about her and were not afraid to ask, especially the strange straw man. Scarecrow, Glinda had called him. There was no end to his inquisitiveness. That became even more apparent when the topic turned to Wonderland.

"You must tell me more. It sounds like a fascinating place." For a man with a face that was clearly fake, he was able to show a great deal of emotion. Alice was mesmerized by the way the cloth of his face stretched as he smiled, greedy for more information.

Alice tried to give him as much as she could, if for no

other reason than to distract herself from the emptiness of the land. She wasn't ready to think about where she was or what she was doing there, so answering Scarecrow's interrogation gave her something to focus on. Glinda, for the most part, remained silent, except to direct them on a new path occasionally. Alice tried to look at her without appearing rude, but Glinda hardly seemed to notice, deep in concentration.

Finally, when Alice thought that she would surely collapse from exhaustion, Glinda pointed to a spot on the horizon. "That is our destination." Following her finger, Alice could barely make out a building of some sort. It was still some distance away, but just having a final destination was enough to give her the energy to make the last of the walk.

As they got closer, the small structure came into focus. It was a small building, only slightly bigger than her parents' bedroom, and made of stone. It had obviously seen its share of hard times, but unlike the old farmhouse, appeared to be mostly intact. Large black stones made up the walls. It didn't look very inviting, but it was more than Alice had seen since she had arrived.

"And what about this Mad Hatter you mentioned? He doesn't sound like a very nice person." Scarecrow pushed the heavy wooden door open with some effort, allowing Glinda and

Alice to pass him.

"He wasn't." Alice wasn't willing to give out any more information on the Hatter at that moment. He was not one of her fonder memories of Wonderland and she had quite enough to handle without bringing him up.

Inside, she let out a deep sigh of relief at the sight of chairs scattered throughout the room. After such a long walk, she would have been perfectly content to sit on the dirt floor to rest, but she was grateful to see that she would not have to. Without waiting for an invitation from either Glinda or Scarecrow, she made her way to the corner where there stood a large chair that looked to be the most comfortable in the room. Sinking into the thickly padded cushions, she released a moan as her feet took a much needed break.

"I'm sorry you had to walk such a long way, Alice. There are other ways to travel through Oz, but they..." Scarecrow stopped, his eyes meeting Glinda's for the briefest of seconds before she looked away towards the other wall. "...aren't always available to us."

Alice didn't have the energy to respond. Once she had fallen into the chair, the last of her strength had left her. Staying awake was an effort. How she longed to curl up and take a nap. She had started her long journey without the benefit of a full night's sleep. And being terrified for such a long period of time

[42]

could be rather taxing on the body. She wondered if she would be allowed a small amount of sleep before having to leave the small shelter.

Glinda had not moved from the spot in the middle of the room. She looked tired, but not in quite the same way that Alice did. Her face was lined with concern and her eyes appeared to be deep in thought. Since the woman was mostly silent, Alice had no way of knowing what weighed on her so heavily. And at that moment, Alice could not concern herself. She was too busy trying to let her body rest.

"Glinda, I should go. They will need to be told about the unexpected result of our actions. They will not be happy that we attempted it in the first place." Scarecrow moved slowly to where Glinda stood, whose eyes drilled into the floor as if they might hold some kind of answers. He put one of his oddly shaped hands on her shoulder. "Will you be okay here?"

Her hand fell on top of his and gave it a small squeeze. "I'll be fine, my friend. You do what you must to cool their anger and make them see this was our only choice."

"It won't be easy. You've been trying to change their minds for a long time. If you haven't gotten through to them by now, I don't know how much success I will have."

For the first time, the smallest hint of a smile graced

Glinda's lips. "If anyone has a chance of success, it is you, Scarecrow. Besides, what's done is done. We cannot go back now."

Their words did not make much sense to Alice, but she was not trying to understand. Her head slowly sank to the arm of the chair as a wave of exhaustion rolled through her entire body. What harm would it cause to rest her eyes for just a moment? Glinda and Scarecrow were lost in conversation with each other and were not giving Alice a second of thought. And she needed to rest. Her eyes began to shut as if weighted down by lead. 'Just for a moment,' she thought.

"I'm sorry, Alice, but there is no time to sleep." Alice nearly jumped out of her chair at Glinda's touch. Had she really dozed off? Judging from the heaviness of her limbs, she doubted it. Even a minute's rest would have felt like a reprieve.

With a strained effort, she forced her aching muscles out of the chair and stood on her bare feet. "Pardon me for being rude, Glinda, but I am so very tired. I was roused from my bed in the middle of the night and brought to this strange place. I don't know what is happening."

"I know you have been through a great deal tonight. You have every right to be tired. I assure you that you will get to rest soon. Just not yet."

Alice's shoulders slumped. Throughout her life, she had

thought herself to be a rather patient person about most things. Perhaps it was her first journey to another world that had brought that out in her. But her patience was running thin. How much more was she going to be asked to endure without some kind of explanation?

"You have questions. I can see them in your eyes. Let's sit and I will attempt to give you any answers that I am able."

She gladly retook her seat. Glinda sat in the chair facing her. Even as tired as she was, Alice had to appreciate how graceful the woman looked in the simple act of sitting. Underneath her blue dress, she crossed her legs at the ankle. Placing her hands in her lap, Glinda smiled and waited.

That was Alice's cue to ask her questions. Oddly, she struggled to form words. It wasn't that she didn't have questions. It was that she had so many, she didn't know where to begin. Looking around the sparse room, her best option seemed to be to start simple. "What is this building?"

Glinda's face relaxed, relieved that she was being handed an easy question first. "This is a simple guardhouse. It is all that remains of the great castle that once belonged to the Wicked Witch of the East. After her defeat, the citizens of Oz thought it best to destroy the fortress instead of using it for some other means. Perhaps they thought that wiping it from the earth would somehow erase the person who owned it from memory."

Judging from her tone, Alice could tell that Glinda had not approved. She, herself, did not have enough information to have an opinion on the matter. If the walls of that castle were the same as the little guardhouse then it must have been a strong place. She could see a valid argument for both sides of the matter.

But, for Alice, that was the end of the simple questions.

"You said that this place was called Oz. I'm afraid that I've never heard of such a place, in my world or in stories. And again, I'm terribly sorry for being rude, but it looks to be a truly dreadful place. If what I have seen is only the beginning, then I think I'd prefer to go home."

The tension quickly returned to Glinda's face. They had reached the type of questioning that she had been expecting from the girl. Alice found herself suddenly fearful of treading into that territory. But she had started and had little choice but to continue.

Glinda pushed herself back in the chair until she sat up straight against its back. "Looking at the world in its present condition, it's easy to forget that it was not always this way. The Land of Oz was once a beautiful place, filled with magical wonders that never ceased to amaze. The people were happy then." Her eyes began to glaze over as if lost in a trance of a better time, the memories of the past running through her vision. And just like that, it passed. Looking directly at Alice, she continued. "That is not to say that we did not have our share of problems. That's the price of magic. It comes with certain darker aspects."

Alice had moved up in her seat until she was nearly at its edge. All sense of tiredness had disappeared from her body as she listened to Glinda's words. Despite the horrors that she had seen in her brief time in Oz, she could not help but feel fascinated by its history. It was the same feeling that she had all those years ago while she sat on a mushroom and Caterpillar told her about Wonderland.

"Witches have been around since long before the beginning of Oz. I am one myself. Some of us have chosen the path of the Good. Others felt the draw of the Wicked. That is merely the course of nature here. For many years, the Witches ruled, each presiding over a territory that they, and they alone, controlled. I, myself, oversaw the South. But then, a wizard came to the land. Traveling in a balloon across the sky, he amazed all of Oz and many called for him to lead. It was found out some years later that he was no wizard at all, just a man relying on tricks and deception to hold on to his power. But before that was known, he brought most of the Witches together and united us. Many, who felt they were no longer needed, slowly moved out of sight and disappeared from our history."

"Where did they go?" Alice hadn't realized she was holding her breath the entire time Glinda was talking until she asked the question and had to catch it.

"No one is quite sure. Some believe that they are still here, in hiding. Some are of the mind that they used their power to leave Oz altogether. And there are some who think that perhaps they just died. But, no matter their fate, we have not heard from them in some time. As for the few of us who remained, we tried to use our powers to the benefit of Oz." Glinda sat up straighter in her chair. Alice could tell that, though she might not look it, she must have been a great witch. She did not need much convincing that Glinda was one of the witches who worked for Good. Could a Wicked Witch have such beauty, as Glinda clearly did, underneath the worry in her face?

"Of the remaining witches, two used their powers to bring discord to the land. The Wicked Witches of the East and West ruled over their territories, harshly, using fear as their main weapon. The Wizard of Oz, being that he had no real power, left the Wicked Witches alone as long as no harm came to the rest of Oz. And that is how we lived for a great many years, until the arrival of Dorothy."

"Dorothy?" Alice sat up excitedly in her chair. "That's the name Scarecrow called me when we first met."

"Yes. She is who we were expecting. Dorothy happened upon our land by accident. She was caught in a tornado, much like the one you saw earlier. That house out there was hers. It was the tool that Dorothy used to kill the Wicked Witch of the East. Yes, it was quite by accident, but the people of Oz chose to look at her as a powerful sorceress who had vanquished one of the great evils of our land. The Wizard used Dorothy to his advantage and sent her to kill the other Wicked Witch, a task that seemed far beyond her means. But despite the odds, she succeeded. And as an added feat, she exposed the false Wizard and persuaded him to leave the land. Her time is what we now call the Fall of the Wicked."

Alice had begun to wring her hands together, eager to hear more. The land that Glinda described sounded enchanting and nothing like the one she found herself in. What had happened to that magical world that it became such a nightmare?

"After her departure from Oz, we went through many changes. Without the Wizard and the Wicked Witches, the people were allowed to thrive in a way they hadn't been able to

[49]

in a very long time. Magic ran through the land. Cities began to expand to sizes never before seen in Oz. It was possibly the most prosperous time in our history, a time worthy of being called the Reign of the Good."

The small amount of sparkle that Glinda had in her eyes during the story faded. "But like most eras of peace and prosperity, it ended swiftly. After what seemed like such a brief time, the Wicked Witch of Oz arrived. No one knows where she came from or how she got here. She may have been here the whole time, waiting for a chance to strike. In the years since she came, she has managed to wrought devastation to every part of Oz."

"Is she a very ugly witch?" Alice felt a little ridiculous for asking that question first. But from all the stories of witches she had read since she was young, she supposed all evil witches were hideous monsters.

"No one can say for sure. She is never without a heavy cloak that conceals her face. The few who have been in her presence and survived to tell of it were never able to get a good look. I, who have come the closest to her of everyone, did not get to see beneath her hood."

A strong clap of thunder sounded outside, causing Alice to jump high in her seat. The boom was so strong it shook the heavy stone walls. Without her attention focused so intently on

Glinda's story, she could hear how much the wind had picked up since they had gotten there. She had to be grateful that they had made it to the building when they did. The weather sounded like it was quickly getting worse, not that it had been all that good since she arrived.

Shaking off her fright, she turned back to Glinda. "You've seen this Witch up close before?"

"I have. I am the only good witch left in Oz. The others went away when the Wizard arrived. When the Witch first started showing her powers, I was the one called. As a protector of Oz, it was my duty to stop her. But I failed. The Witch was able to defeat me, shattering my scepter in the process. I was left next to powerless and she was able to go on and do untold damage."

"You could have been killed."

"I very nearly was. For reasons only known to her, the Witch stopped the fight just short of ending my life." Glinda looked away, eyeing a layer of dirt in the corner of the room. "There are times I wish she had finished the job. Then I would not have to see what Oz has become because of my failure."

Alice fought with the emotions roiling inside her. Many different feelings, most of them contradictory, flooded her mind. Fear. Curiosity. Amazement. Concern. Shock. She knew that, for anyone else, it might be a stretch to believe. Wonderland had given her a broader mind that was more willing to accept such strange occurrences. But Alice was at a loss as to understand her role in the whole affair.

"I'm truly sorry for all that you have endured, but I know nothing about this land. How could I possibly be of any help?"

Glinda put on a comforting smile, trying to ease Alice's troubled expression. "Oz's magic has always been vulnerable to those from the Other World, like Dorothy and the Wizard. Because of that, I think you will be able to defeat the Witch."

Alice sat up in her chair, forcing her back into the cushions. "Me? Defeat the Witch? You can't be serious. I'm just a girl. What do I know of fighting witches?"

Glinda stood, towering over the girl, but not in an intimidating way. Her smile was still soft even though it was obviously a mask. "In Oz, a mere girl is capable of more than you could possibly imagine."

Alice remained less than convinced. She knew Glinda was trying to be comforting, even encouraging, but it wasn't enough. They were talking about taking down a witch, a powerful one at that. What powers did she have to match what she would be facing? "I wouldn't even know where to begin."

"That one's easy, dear." Glinda took her hands and

pulled her to her feet. With soft fingers, she pushed a lock of brown hair from Alice's eyes. "First, you must meet with the Great and Terrible Council of Oz."

Chapter 4

"You were told not to even attempt another Calling, but as always, you did exactly what you wanted to do." The tall man's voice echoed throughout the hall. He stood on top of a curved dais with three other people who did not appear very comfortable to be in his company. Judging from his tone of voice, he was a terribly unpleasant man.

"That's Syrdip. He's the Council Representative of Northern Oz, Gillikin Country." Scarecrow leaned over in his chair to whisper to Alice.

The girl was in shock as she witnessed the council meeting. For what she could tell, it did not appear to be much of a civilized council. There had been more screaming than talking, most of it coming from Syrdip. It made Alice think of a time when her father had taken her to Christ Church to attend a faculty meeting. She really had no place there but was curious to discover the details of such things. After much pestering, her father finally agreed. What she witnessed there was very much the same as the meeting in front of her. How could they expect to get anything done if all they were willing to do was argue?

Glinda stood before the raised council members,

managing to keep her stance under their staring eyes. "As I have tried to make you understand many times, I have always felt that this was our best hope at a positive outcome. The Witch has proven to be more powerful than anything we have fought before." Despite the harshness of how she was being spoken to, Glinda remained as composed as when Alice first met her. She showed no sign that Syrdip's assault had affected her at all.

"That is exactly why we shouldn't be wasting our precious few magical resources on summoning idiot girls from the Other Land." Alice felt insulted. Syrdip hadn't even been introduced to her and he was already calling her names. She felt inclined to say something and might just have if it had not been for Scarecrow's hand grabbing hold of her arm. She tried to calm herself, but seethed underneath the surface.

"I'm sure my fellow council member did not mean to show such disrespect to our guest." A soft spoken voice interrupted whatever angry words Syrdip was about to say. It came from a smaller woman sitting to the right side of the dais. Alice had a hard time looking away. It was not every day that she saw a woman who was not only shorter than herself, but with a head of lavender hair that fell to her shoulders. She had to look very carefully, but she was sure she could see a lavender tint to the woman's skin. "Emotions have been running high for quite some time now, but that is no reason to be outright vicious."

Scarecrow leaned over again and whispered, "Lindell is the representative from what little is left of Eastern Oz, Munchkin Country. She tries her best to control Syrdip's temper, but she does not always succeed. Sometimes it takes more than calm words to reign in his anger."

Lindell's words did seem to calm the mood, at least temporarily. Syrdip's tone became strained, as if it was an effort for him to speak calmly.

The council meeting continued on, but Alice's attention began to wander. From her chair next to the dais, she had a clear view of the entire hall. She could tell that it had once been part of a much bigger room, but a pile of large rocks had made the rest unusable. That would also explain the very large hole in the ceiling that Alice could see dark purple clouds through. There was not a very large audience, maybe a third of the seats were occupied with various types of people.

Alice did not feel comfortable. Almost every eye in the room seemed to be on her and had been ever since she and Glinda had entered. Granted, she might also have stared if anyone had made the entrance that they had. It could not be often that the audience watched a massive bubble float down from the roof and deposit two people in the center of the room.

Before leaving the stone guardhouse, Glinda said the council would not be happy to see her. She gave no explanation as to the reason that they would be so upset, and Alice didn't feel it necessary to ask. But Glinda did stress that no matter their reaction, it was of the utmost importance that Alice get to the meeting as quickly as possible. "Even if I have to drain my limited magic to accomplish it."

In Alice's life, she had enjoyed her fair share of surprises, but none could compare with traveling with Glinda. One second they were standing on the ground and the next they were being lifted in the air by a clear bubble. Alice watched as the land got further and further away from her feet. "It's okay, dear. I used to travel this way all the time. It's quite safe."

She wished she could have felt as confident as Glinda had sounded, but that was a difficult task. When she looked down and saw the earth miles below her feet with only a thin layer of clear bubble to keep her from falling to it, she began to have her doubts. Alice had dreamt many times about what it would be like to fly without riding Gryphon, but they were just dreams. When faced with the reality, she found that it gave her quite a scare, one that even Glinda was not able to calm.

Through the bubble, Alice was able to see the land speeding below her. There was a lot of land, but not much to it.

[57]

As hard as she tried, she could not imagine what the place looked like before the Witch had gotten her hands on it. Glinda tried to tell her about the towns and monuments that used to stand, but Alice could not picture them. All she saw before her was a devastation from which there seemed to be no return.

"Where are we going?" Alice had asked, though she was distracted by the forest of dead looking trees below them.

"We are going to the northern region of Oz. It is one of the least affected areas of the country, so the citizens tend to migrate there. It's the Council's chosen meeting ground."

Alice began to see scattered debris haphazardly thrown across the ground. Some pieces of rubble were as big as her house while others were much smaller. With no discernable pattern, it seemed as if the clouds had decided to rain stones instead of water. "What is that?"

Another sad look crossed Glinda's face. "That is the remains of the main highway. Once yellow bricks stretched all through the country, making a road that connected all of Oz together. Parts of it still stand, but with huge gaps torn through it. The Witch destroyed large portions, but most of it was blown apart by the tornados that plague this region."

Alice tried to imagine what it must be like for Glinda. How would she feel if she had to walk through the streets of Oxford and see everything she knew in shambles? What if her

[58]

beloved spot by the river had been reduced to nothing but a smoking hole? Would she be able to look at it every day and not break down into tears?

"I must warn you, Alice. The Council's anger will be great. It will mostly be at me, but you will most likely have to suffer some of it. You should prepare yourself."

"But why? Who is this Great and Terrible Council anyway?"

"After his departure, the Wizard placed Scarecrow in charge of the country. It did not take long for everyone, himself included, to realize that it was too large a task. Scarecrow has an inquisitive mind, much better suited for studying the little things he finds so fascinating. Running the entirety of Oz was beyond his capability. So the Council was formed. Representatives from the four corners of the land were elected to serve and together they ran the government. For a while, it was an ideal solution. But then the Witch arrived and, like everything, the Council changed."

Those were the last words Glinda spoke on the journey. They floated their way through the air in complete silence. Several times, Alice was tempted to speak, just for the sound, but she thought better of it. From Glinda's expression, she looked to be preparing herself mentally. Alice thought it best to leave the woman alone with her thoughts. Answers would come soon enough, she was sure.

"I'm not sure what the purpose of us meeting with you today is, Glinda. By all accounts, your experiment was a failure."

Alice was brought back to herself by a new voice. It came from a third person sitting on the dais. The man had dark olive skin that was only marked by a jet black tattoo of some sort. It started at his neck, twisted across his skin, and continued down until it was lost in his loose fitting shirt.

"And who is that man?" She whispered to Scarecrow. She could only hope that her voice would not be heard. But with so many people staring at her, that couldn't be certain.

"He is the representative from the Western Winkie country. No one knows his name. Some say he doesn't even have one. He was born during the reign of the Wicked Witch of the West. Rumor has it that she did not allow her slaves to name their children because families were not together long. The truth is unclear because he refuses to speak of his past."

Glinda took a step closer to the Council. "I do not believe that my experiment, as you call it, was a failure. True, my hope has always been to call Dorothy back to Oz. In all my previous attempts, no one has answered the call. I thought it was because I no longer possessed the magic necessary to reach the Other Land. But now, I know that is not the case. I can only

[60]

assume that my other Callings were successful as well, but for some reason, Dorothy is unable to answer."

"But who is this girl? We know nothing about her. From your own words, she doesn't even appear to know Dorothy. How can you call this a success?" Syrdip's words began to climb in volume. Any calm that Lindell was able to bring out in him was quickly evaporating.

"Her name is Alice. It would be quite rude to continue calling her "this girl". She has been nothing but respectful since her arrival and should be shown the same courtesy, don't you agree?"

"I'm sure Syrdip meant no disrespect." Lindell raised her voice, asserting her own authority on the Council, though it kept its softness. Alice found herself liking the smaller woman. She was clearly the more reasonable council member.

Syrdip, however, did not look at all happy with the interruption. There was no doubt he meant every bit of disrespect that had come from his mouth. It was clear that he was accustomed to being the leader and did not appreciate anyone else trying to take over. "Nothing changes the fact that you wasted valuable magic on this endeavor. That you brought this...Alice...to Oz means very little. How can we expect her to be successful at fighting the Witch where so many have failed?"

[61]

"Did anyone expect Dorothy to bring about the Fall of the Wicked?" How Glinda was able to maintain her composure under such an aggressive interrogation was beyond Alice. To her, only criminals should receive such treatment. What had Glinda done to warrant such cruelty?

"That is exactly your problem, Glinda. You expect the people of Oz to sit back and wait for another Act of Dorothy to save us. That time is over. We must take matters into our own hands and devise a plan of attack."

His words were met with a cheer from the watching crowd. With everyone's attention focused on the council members, Alice was finally able to scan the audience. It really was the strangest grouping that she had ever seen. Some were tall and thin, others short and round. Their skin color varied from pale white to dark brown, even a couple with a green tint.

It was the full grown tiger that made her stop. Not because the large cat sat in his chair like a human, but because of who was sitting next to it. He was a younger man, not much older than Alice from the look of him, with short, jet black hair. Alice couldn't stop staring at his eyes. They were so grey they appeared silver. Unlike everyone else in the audience, he was not looking at the Council, but at her.

His gaze chilled Alice to the bone. A shiver ran through her. It reminded her of the feeling she had back in her room just before being dragged into the mirror. He wasn't just staring at her, but through her. She found that she did not care for the feeling one bit and, therefore, was not very fond of the young man.

"I agree that we should be forming our own plans to take on this enemy. But it would be foolish not to realize that we may not be up to the challenge. In the years since the Witch has risen to power, she has easily defeated all of our efforts. On top of her considerable might, she has taken many of the Winkie citizens under her control." As Glinda spoke, she cast a quick glance at the unnamed member of the council, who quickly looked away. "Because of that, we must explore alternate solutions."

Alice was having a hard time paying attention. The meeting didn't seem to be very productive anyway. Her mother always accused her of having a wandering mind when it came to things that others found to be so important. But she couldn't focus on anything but the silver eyes drilling into her. Was it mere curiosity causing him to look at her that way?

His stare finally broke when the tiger put a massive paw on his shoulder. As soon as the eyes looked away, Alice felt an overwhelming sense of relief. She let out a breath that she hadn't been aware she was holding. Without the distraction, she was able to turn back to the Council.

She leaned closer to Scarecrow again. "What about the fourth person up there? She seems not to have much to say." She was looking at a short, round woman who was almost as wide as she was tall. Alice thought she appeared rather distorted, like a reflection in a warped mirror.

"Her name is Cantu. She comes from the South, Quadling Country. One of the first things the Witch did was transform the impassable desert that surrounds all of Oz into a violent ocean. The entire southern part of the land flooded. It happened so quickly, and with such force, that the Quadlings had no chance to escape. Cantu is one of the only survivors. Since she was found, she has not spoken a single word. The poor thing must be completely traumatized."

Alice had a hard time imagining that much land flooded and that many lives lost. At home, the river would occasionally overflow its banks, but that was only after hours of heavy rain. And then, it was only a bit of a nuisance to deal with, nothing like what Scarecrow described. She had to wonder if the Witch knew what her actions would cause when she changed the sand into water.

"I beg the Council to reconsider their position on my plan. It is our best option at this moment in time. I sincerely believe that it can bring an end to our years of hardship." Glinda was at the end of her argument. She had presented all that she could. Her only hope was that her plea was enough to sway their minds. "And," she paused, "if you cannot agree with this course of action, then I am prepared to proceed without your approval."

Tension radiated through the room as Syrdip's eyes flashed with anger. A scowl, deeper than the one he already wore set on his face. Even the other Council members squirmed uncomfortably in their seats.

"Is that so, Glinda?" Syrdip's voice was louder than it had ever been, echoing against the stone walls. Alice didn't believe she had ever seen a person that angry before. "And what good do you imagine that will accomplish?" Slowly, he got to his feet, his knuckles turning white as he gripped the dais. He towered over Glinda even more. It was a blatantly threatening move. "You have already failed once in your task of protecting this land. Do you honestly believe that the people of Oz will be willing to put their hopes and safety in the hands of the blond in the bubble?" Pure contempt stained his words.

The insult's effect was immediate. Glinda's spine stiffened, causing her to stand straight. It somehow made her look taller and more majestic than before. Her hair and dress began to blow in a wind that couldn't be felt by anyone else. "I am Glinda the Good." Her voice echoed throughout the room, magically amplified. "I have been a protector of Oz since long before anyone in this room was born. You may have turned your backs on the old ways. You may not even believe in me. But you will show me the respect that I am due. Throughout this Council's reign, I have tried not to overstep my bounds and let the people's chosen government have their say. Do not make me regret that decision. My magic may be limited, but it is still within my power to impose my will."

Alice was startled to see that Glinda's feet were no longer touching the floor. She floated close to a foot off the ground. Her dress flapped against her ankles, caught in the magical wind. Instinctively, Alice moved back in her chair to get further away. From what she could tell, she was not the only one doing so.

Glinda slowly sank back down to the floor. The phantom wind settled until there was no trace of it. Glinda gazed at the shaken Council with the same calm expression that had never left her face. Not even Syrdip said anything in answer to her threat.

"Let her try." The response didn't come from the dais, but from the audience instead. Alice turned, with everyone else, to find who had spoken. She hadn't expected to see the gray-eyed young man standing in front of his seat. He did not look at anyone other than the Council, his face stern. "What harm could it do? Glinda has already brought Alice here. There must be some reason that the Calling worked as it did."

Without waiting for any sort of acknowledgement, he sat and whispered a few words to the tiger.

Glinda turned her head slightly, looking at the young man from the corner of her eye. "Thank you, Brax."

Everyone spoke about Alice as if she weren't there. She had tried to listen patiently, but she had had enough. "Excuse me. I'm sorry to interrupt." She stood, ignoring the audience as they all turned towards her. She could feel those silver eyes staring at her. "But do I not have a say in this matter at all?"

Syrdip gave an angry scoff in her direction before looking away, too disgusted to maintain eye contact. He directed his next words at Lindell. "This is exactly what I'm talking about. Glinda brought this girl here, giving us the impression that she had agreed. Now she wants a say? Should we allow her to make this foolish attempt, only to have the child change her mind in the middle of it?"

"For Ozma's sake, Syrdip, would you let Alice speak before flying off the handle? Your outbursts have grown quite tiresome." Lindell had apparently reached the end of her patience, no longer willing to be the Council's peacemaker.

"Thank you." Alice stepped forward until she stood next to Glinda. She wanted to sneak a glance at the woman, perhaps get a reassuring nod, but she knew it was probably not wise to look away from the Council. "I did not say I was changing my mind, sir. I am willing to help in any way I can. But since I have arrived in this place, no one has bothered to tell me what it is I am expected to do."

Syrdip's face lit up with a satisfied smirk. He opened his mouth, an insult surely about to be spoken, but a sharp wave of Lindell's hand stopped him.

"In all the confusion, we have forgotten that you know very little of our land. Glinda must have informed you about some of what has occurred here. But with the speed that she brought you to us, there could not have been enough time to cover details. We apologize for this."

Without another word, Lindell pushed away from the dais and moved to the back wall. She was quickly followed by the other Council members. They huddled together and began talking in whispers. Alice could make out very little of what was said, but she could distinguish Syrdip's angry whisper above the rest.

"You did well." Glinda gave her a small smile. "That should carry some favor."

Alice was unclear on what exactly she had done well.

[68]

Other than finally speaking up over listening to the Council talk about her as if she were not in the room, she had not done much. She was about to ask how her few words could have swayed the Council, when Glinda had been unable to do so. Her display of magic should have been much more successful than Alice's meager words. She did not get a chance to ask her question, however, because she was interrupted by someone clearing their throat.

The Council had returned to their places on the dais while Alice was distracted by her own thoughts. It was the Winkie who brought her back to the present.

"The Council has discussed the matter before us today." His voice rang clearly throughout the room, the audience having gone silent. "By a majority ruling, we have decided to give our consent to Glinda's plan. We will allow her and Alice to see it through."

The entire audience began clamoring at the same time. Hushed and hurried whispers mixed with angry proclamations. The people did not seem to be of one mind concerning the decision. Before the crowd could grow in volume, the Winkie raised his hand for silence.

"We will offer what assistance we can, but will allow Glinda full authority in her actions."

[69]

Glinda beamed at the Council. Whether because of their decision or the fact she would not have to follow through on her threat, Alice could not be sure. But she did notice the look that Glinda shared with Syrdip. There were many things in that exchange, but it most resembled a long standing hatred near its boiling point.

"I am grateful to the Council for agreeing with me and for your gracious offer of assistance. It is my sincere hope to not impose on your generosity. For now, my only request is that since Alice has agreed to help us in our greatest time of need, the least we can do is permit her to wear the shoes."

Another outburst from the crowd followed. Alice was shocked at the heated response. Of all the things that were said in the Council meeting, talk of shoes seemed to be the most innocent. The reaction from the people made Glinda's request sound beyond scandalous. There was little time for Alice to process the reason for it before Syrdip's voice boomed over the rabble.

"Let her wear the blasted things then." The ugly sneer on his face made Alice uncomfortable. There was too much malice in his words for her to imagine he was not wishing her harm. "They should go lovely with her attire."

Alice looked down. She could feel heat begin to rise in her cheeks as, for the first time, she realized that she had sat through the entire meeting still wearing her white nightgown.

Chapter 5

"These shoes are one of Oz's greatest relics, once thought lost to us forever."

Glinda had lead Alice out of the meeting hall through a side door. They moved so quickly that Scarecrow barely had time to assure them he would be waiting when they were finished. Alice followed through a series of twisting hallways, each one looking grimmer than the one before. She considered trying to discuss what had just taken place, but she thought better of it. Most of her attention was focused on trying to keep pace with Glinda.

The second they had been dismissed from the Council's presence, Glinda's entire demeanor changed. The soft smile and calm appearance vanished. They were replaced by a barely concealed rage. Alice had to wonder about the woman's ability to cover her true emotions when she wanted. Was it possible to completely trust a person who had that skill?

But, despite her doubts, she followed Glinda through the halls. It made little sense for her to turn back, especially after the meeting. She had made a promise, not only to Glinda, but to the entire Council and all the members of the audience.

As long as it was in her power, she would live up to that promise. Alice had never been the type to go back on her word, unless it was absolutely necessary.

After making a sixth or seventh turn, Alice had been unable to keep track in their haste, they walked through a set of double doors and into a richly decorated room. From what she had seen of the state of the land, she did not think it possible for such a room to exist. It was filled with the finest of furnishings. Chairs were made with a luxurious material that Alice had never seen or felt before in her life. Art, that looked both old and priceless, hung on the walls in gilded frames. The lush carpet tickled her toes as her feet sank into it. It was a room that befit royalty.

Glinda wasted no time, moving swiftly across the room and opening a wardrobe that sat against one the curtained windows. From there she pulled an ornate wooden box. Intricate designs were carved into every surface of the wood. Alice could tell that it contained something incredibly valuable. It was from the box that Glinda pulled out the shoes.

Alice had to blink a couple of times to fully process the sight of them. The shoes were, by far, the most magnificent pair that she had ever seen. They were of a simple design, with a small heel that measured maybe an inch. They were made so that the wearer merely had to slip them on. Alice had many pairs similar, but none that compared to the ones in front of her.

Even in the dimly lit room, they shone brightly, sparkling with red, green, and white light. Jewels adorned the shoe's surface, artfully arranged into a complex pattern of swirls and spirals. It most resembled vines reaching out to encompass them. Beneath the shining jewels, Alice could see a silver material that shone just as brightly. She brought a hand forward to touch them, but stopped herself with her fingers inches away.

"It's okay to touch them. They have been through much worse, I assure you." The anger that Alice had seen on Glinda's face had seemed to recede once again, like the shoes somehow erased those thoughts from her mind. She couldn't be sure of how real it was, but Glinda looked almost serene holding them in her hands.

She received an answer the second her hand touched the shoes. A sense of calm washed over her entire body. She could feel the doubts and worries that she had been holding onto since arriving melt away as if they were nothing. Magic pulsed beneath her fingertips with a power that made Alice shiver.

"What are these?" Her voice came out as barely a

whisper. If Glinda had not been standing right next to her, she would not have heard Alice's words. But the sense of awe she was feeling prohibited her from talking any louder.

"They are one of the great relics of Oz, one of the objects in this world that has magic all of its own, without outside assistance." Glinda placed the shoes on a small table next to one of the couches. They illuminated the area around them. "No one is quite sure of their origin. They have been around longer than living memory. Some believe they once belonged to the mythical fairy queen, Lurline, the founder of Oz, and they were passed to her daughter, Ozma, after. But, like I said, no one can be sure."

Glinda placed a gentle hand on Alice's back and led her to a chair. Her mind was focused on Glinda's words, but she could not tear her eyes away from the shoes. They were completely entrancing.

"We do know that they have passed through our history, from person to person. The last one to wear them was Dorothy herself. When she left Oz, we feared that she had taken them with her and they were lost to us. But one day, not long after the transformation of the desert, they were found washed up on the shores of Munchkin Country. They were in great disrepair when they were discovered. I was able to use rubies,

[75]

emeralds, and diamonds to restore what I could of them. We have kept their existence hidden ever since. If the Witch were to learn that we had them, she would surely try to take them for herself. That must not be allowed."

Alice shifted uncomfortably in her seat. "But you told the Council that you wanted me to wear them? Is that such a wise choice? What if the Witch managed to take them from me?"

"No need to worry about that, dear. After I place a small charm on them, no one will be able to remove them from your feet."

Carefully, Glinda reached down and took a hold of Alice's left leg. Picking up one of the shoes, she gently slid it onto her foot. The second shoe was soon to follow. As soon as both of them were on, Alice felt an energy coursing through them. Glinda waved one hand over the shoes and they began to glow even brighter than before.

"They fit perfectly," Alice said with more than a hint of astonishment.

The woman gave a small laugh. Something was off about the sound, like it was something that she may have forgotten how to do. "Yes. That is just one of the magical qualities they possess. It comes in quite handy since we are never sure who might wear them next."

When Glinda had finished casting the spell, she got to her feet and began walking around the room. She scanned all of the grand objects placed neatly around as a sad look passed across her face. Alice didn't want to interrupt her thoughts, but she knew it was necessary to do so before too much time had passed.

"What is your plan, Glinda? You've told me what needs to be done, but you haven't given me any information as to how to accomplish such a seemingly impossible task."

She watched as the woman's shoulders fell deeply. "This isn't the first time, and will most likely not be the last, that I must ask for your forgiveness, Alice. Your arrival was unexpected. I did not anticipate having to explain so much. I've told you that it was Dorothy that we were trying to summon."

Alice moved slowly until she stood behind Glinda. "And from what I could tell, it was not your first attempt."

"No." Glinda turned. The sad look still haunted her features. "It was the last of many failed attempts to perform the Calling. As you've seen, it has not made me very popular amongst the people. But it is my strongest belief that someone from the Other World is the key to my plans. In the absence of Dorothy, you are my only hope to prove it."

"But how?" It was hard for Alice to keep the impatience

from her voice, but it almost seemed as if Glinda was intentionally being elusive.

"There are four ancient relics of Oz. You already wear one of them." Glinda gestured to Alice's feet. "Like the shoes, they are all believed to have mythical origins that stretch all the way back to Lurline and the founding of Oz. They possess the oldest and deepest magic found in the entire land. It has been said that if the four objects are brought together, they will allow the collector access to that magic. But it's strong, a power that has never been fully seen in Oz before. Only a truly special person will be able to control it."

"That's why you need someone from my world?"

"Like I told you before, Oz's magic has always been vulnerable to those from the Other World. I believe that someone from there, like yourself, can harness the power that these objects will bring forth."

While Glinda's plan was becoming more apparent, there was still one detail that nagged Alice. "You say you believe that these objects are the key to this great magical power, and you also think that I will be able to control it. It sounds like a great deal of your plan is based on speculation and rumor. Is that why the Council did not consent to your actions?"

Again, Glinda's temperament changed, anger distorting her face. "The Council prohibits me because they are unable to let go of any amount of authority they hold. When they first came to power, they ran a fair system of government, taking advice from any wise person who would offer it. I was one of their most loyal advisors. As time went on, however, they began to see me and others as threats. They somehow forgot Oz's past and concerned themselves only with being seen as the true rulers of the land. In most cases, they have completely forgotten the old ways and only summon me when they see magic as their only recourse."

From her tone, Alice could hear many different emotions running through Glinda's voice. There was definitely anger, mixed with sadness and perhaps regret as well. It was not hard to see where they all came from. Glinda had once been an important figure in Oz and she had been pushed aside, mostly likely at Syrdip's insistence. Thinking that did not help Alice's impression of the despicable man.

As quickly as her anger appeared, it passed. Glinda waved her hand through the air as if banishing any unpleasant thoughts. "Let's not give another minute of our time to that ridiculous Council. They may have given their approval, but they will surely try to interfere at every opportunity. It's best to make a habit of ignoring their existence and focusing on the task at hand."

Alice wished ignoring the Council and their words was simple, but clearly, Glinda had much more practice than her. She had a quite annoying habit of letting thoughts roll around in her head, no matter how hard she tried not to. But, she did recognize that in order for her job to be over, then she'd have to try very hard. Because from what Glinda was describing, they had a lot of work to do.

"Where do we start?" It bothered her a little that Glinda was being so vague. Why was the plan only coming out in small amounts, instead of her just telling her what needed to be done?

"The first thing we must do is travel back to where we began. Not far from where we first met stands a dying forest. In the middle of the trees, there is a small cottage that used to belong to a dear friend of mine. Hiding inside is what remains of my magic scepter. I have kept it there ever since the Witch shattered it in battle because no one has visited it for many years."

"Why must we collect the broken pieces of a magic wand? What use will it be?"

"It's not the scepter itself we are after. Embedded in the staff's head is a diamond, once called Oz's Eye. It is one of the relics. I was able to obtain the diamond a long time ago and kept it with me at all times. But with my scepter broken, it was no longer safe. That is why I chose to hide it."

"Even if it's hidden well, couldn't the Witch have somehow discovered its location?"

Glinda moved away from Alice, towards one of the heavily curtained windows. Pushing the material aside, she peered out into the dark light of the sky. "That is our one great advantage in this endeavor. The Witch seems to have no knowledge of these relics. If she did, I believe she would have gone after them long ago. And besides, even if she did collect them, she would most likely not be able to control the power they would unleash, not in the way I am certain you could."

"Because you believe only someone from my world has that ability?"

"Precisely, my dear. An Ozian could wield it I'm sure, but they wouldn't be able to control it for long."

Alice took a second to consider that there was a time in her life when she would have felt strange saying something like "my world". She had always been a curious child with a wild imagination, but it was her trip to Wonderland that opened her mind to all the possibilities that the world, and many other worlds, had to offer. What would her younger self say if she could tell her about all the things she had seen? Would that little girl believe it without having seen it for herself?

"If we are to travel to various parts of Oz, am I meant to do so in my nightgown?" Syrdip's nasty remark about her attire still stung long after she should have let it pass.

"Of course not. I'm sorry it has taken me so long to think of it. If I had known just how hostile Syrdip would be towards you, I never would have brought you there in your current condition." She stood facing Alice, so close that the girl could smell the sweetness of her breath. "Let's see what we can come up with."

Soft lights of the palest blue began to form and swirl around Glinda's hand. They danced in front of Alice's eyes like mystical fairies. With a flick of her fingers, Glinda sent the small lights flying towards Alice. She tried to follow them with her eyes as they circled her, but as they began to move faster they became nothing but a blur. Even though she couldn't feel them, the lights began to attach themselves to her nightgown. More and more came until she could no longer see any part of the white material because it was blocked by the growing lights.

For a brief moment, Alice glowed so brightly that she was forced to shut her eyes. Even then, it was not enough to block out the intensity. She expected to feel her skin burning because surely, something so bright had to be hot as well. But it did not. In fact, her arms felt quite cool as a tickling sensation ran up them. She felt like a star, fallen to earth.

When the light started to dim, leaving spots floating in her vision, Alice was astonished at the eerily familiar sight that greeted her. Gone was her nightgown, replaced by a dress made of material softer than even the finest silk she had ever touched. The color, an intensely vibrant blue, almost seemed to pulse, as if it had a life of its own. The white of the pinafore tied around her waist was so pristine that it hurt her eyes to look directly at it. The comfort she felt from its shocking similarities to the dress she had worn all those years ago in Wonderland was shaken only by its garish beauty.

How could Glinda possibly produce a near perfect replica of her old dress without ever having seen it before?

"Much better, don't you think?" Glinda appraised her creation, nodding in approval. "My powers may not be what they once were, but there are still some areas of magic that I excel at."

Since arriving in Oz, she had seen Glinda do some most impressive things. If that came from only a small fraction of her powers, Alice wasn't sure she wanted to see her at her strongest. Not for the first time, Alice thought there might be more to Glinda than met the eye.

Chapter 6

"Can you tell me about Dorothy?"

Glinda sighed, pushing her fingertips into her forehead. Alice recognized the signs of frustration. She had seen them many times before. But, unlike most people, Glinda didn't even try to disguise her irritation. "My dear, other than Scarecrow, I don't think I have ever met such an overwhelmingly inquisitive person."

Alice could have easily been offended by the comment, but she wasn't. She had become so accustomed to other's exacerbation with her that it no longer bothered her. Besides, why shouldn't she ask questions? How else was she to learn what she needed to know about Oz and the Witch? If she was going to be expected to defeat a powerful enemy, shouldn't she be armed with as much knowledge as possible?

Scarecrow, however, did seem genuinely affronted. His face showed as much indignation as it was able. "What is wrong with being inquisitive?"

"There is nothing wrong with it." Glinda sighed again, regretting having said anything at all. "I did not mean to imply otherwise."

[84]

"I should think not," Scarecrow said, rather huffily. "It was you who encouraged me to use my brains, after all. What was it that you said? 'The Wizard may not have been able to give you real brains, but that doesn't stop you from using the ones that you never knew you always had.'"

"I have apologized, my friend. I should have thought before I spoke."

Scarecrow looked away, but was clearly still offended. He continued to mutter, but he did not seem inclined to share his thoughts with the others. That was just fine with Alice for she was much too tired to concern herself. Glinda showed little care as well. The long trip had taken its toll on both Glinda and Alice. Scarecrow, however, was as energetic as the minute they left, several hours before. Alice guessed it was one of the benefits of being stuffed with straw.

They were walking through what must have once been a field. Strewn in their path were long dead stalks of corn. Most were almost completely rotted, but a few stubbornly held on to their shape, refusing to leave the world completely. They had been crossing the same field for quite some time and Alice still could not see the other side. It stretched for miles and miles.

Alice turned her attention away from what was beginning to look like an endless journey and back to her original question. "So Dorothy? I've heard her name mentioned many times, but no one has said very much about her, other than that she defeated the Wicked Witches."

Instead of sighing again, Glinda looked to the horizon, her eyes scanning the dark purple clouds that loomed ahead. "Dorothy is an important part of Oz's history. Her arrival was one of the great turning points in our destiny, rivaling the coming and going of the Wizard and the reign of the Witches. Her time in Oz changed everything, for good or ill, depending on who you ask."

"For ill? But she caused the Fall of the Wicked, didn't she?"

"Yes, she did. And for that, she is celebrated by everyone. But some also see her as the one who caused the Wizard to abandon the land. There are some, especially in the Northern Gillikin regions, that have never lost faith, believing that he was Oz's true savior. They do not trust my claims that he was a fraud. And there are some, like Syrdip, who believe that Dorothy was merely a simple girl who got lucky. She not only saved our land, but she divided it as well."

Having something to listen to made Alice forget how weary she was from the long trek through the field. "It doesn't sound to me like Oz was all that united to begin with."

"Perhaps not, with the Witches ruling their own small

portions of the country and then the Wizard attempting to rule over everyone from the Emerald City. But, at least, the people all strived for a common goal. When Dorothy returned home, the Council was formed to be the embodiment of the people's desire. As you have seen, that is no longer the case. But then again, not all of us in Oz want the same things anymore. Some place the blame for that on Dorothy's shoulders."

"And that's just not true. Dorothy was a hero." Scarecrow had come out of his foul mood long enough to interject into the conversation. "Anyone who says otherwise has no idea what they're talking about." With the level of anger in his voice, Alice wondered if he had been having the same argument for years.

"What about Dorothy herself? I've heard about what she's done, but I know nothing of her."

"She was a special child. I could tell that just from the short time that I met with her. Other than that, I didn't know much of her myself. I can tell you my impressions of her from our interactions together, but if you want to know more personal information, it is Scarecrow that you want to ask. He was with her on her journey through Oz."

Scarecrow walked alongside Glinda, his offense seemingly forgotten. His steps were clumsy and awkward, like a child just getting used to his legs. Alice supposed it must be like that for all people who are made of straw, but since she had never met one before, she had no kind of reference. "Oh yes, I spent a great deal of time with Dorothy, more than anyone else in Oz, in fact. We got to know each other very well."

"Then what was she like?" Alice was getting tired of asking the same question repeatedly. Why was it so difficult to get an answer out of anyone? She was reminded of her conversations with the Cheshire Cat. Could he have originally come from Oz?

"She was a very brave girl and a true friend. There were times during our travels that I had trouble keeping up, but she never left me behind. And when things got really dangerous, she risked herself to make sure that I was okay. She was that way with all of us."

"All of you? There were more of you?"

"Yes. Four of us made the journey through Oz. Dorothy, myself, Lion, and the Tin Woodman. She found us all on the road and helped us. If it weren't for her, I would probably still be hanging on that pole in this very field. But she would not let that happen. It was just her way. When she saw someone in need of help, she couldn't deny them. Like Glinda said, she was a very special person. Although, her dog was a tad bit annoying."

Alice was so caught up in listening to Scarecrow that she didn't see the small hole in front of her. She stepped right into it, her heel catching and almost sending her to the ground. The sparkling shoes were not the best for such a long journey. She wondered if perhaps Dorothy had the same trouble in her day. "Where are the others?"

Glinda and Scarecrow shared a dark look. Neither of them appeared eager to answer. Several moments of tense silence passed before Glinda turned to Alice. "We don't talk of their fate much. They have been gone for many years now. Lion, who moved to the Quadling Country, was killed when the floods hit the South. Nick Chopper, the Tin Woodman, had taken over leadership of Winkie Country. He was residing in the castle of the Wicked Witch of the West when the new Witch came to power. He has not been heard from since. We can only fear the worst."

Silence lapsed over them. From the way they avoided making eye contact with her and each other, Alice could tell there would be no more conversations on the subject. Even though there were still a million more questions waiting to be asked, she kept them to herself, allowing them to have their thoughts.

Instead, she focused on the walk ahead of her. She

[89]

searched the ground intently for any more holes that might cause her to trip. It had taken a couple of hours, but she had gotten used to walking in the small heels, something she hadn't had much chance to practice in her life. Though there were still times when she'd step wrong and feel her ankle turning. Luckily, she had always managed to right herself and not cause herself any harm. But she figured it was only a matter of time.

She wished they could travel in the bubble that Glinda had used before, but she was told it wasn't possible. "Traveling in that manner requires a great deal of magic, especially for multiple people. I fear I may have overtaxed myself today. When I have the strength, we will surely use it, but until then, we must settle for the old fashioned way."

Alice had hoped to get a couple hours sleep before departing, but Glinda was insistent on setting off immediately. She didn't argue, but she was unsure how she was going to keep going as tired as she was. She also couldn't imagine how Glinda herself was still pressing on. The woman's longer dress had to be a hindrance to her walking. Signs of wear had started to show on Glinda's face, but still she would not pause for even the briefest rest.

Without the benefit of conversation to distract her, Alice's attention became consumed with the cracked ground they walked over. Every once in a while a small creature would dart across their path, scurrying out of sight as quickly as they appeared. One time a tiny animal stopped and stood on its hind legs, staring straight at them. It was nothing more than an ordinary field mouse. Seeing mice running about was not an altogether unusual sight. What struck Alice as odd was that it appeared to be wearing the tattered remains of a dress and a small beat up tiara. Before she could mention it, however, the mouse scampered off, burying itself in the dead corn stalks as it went.

The Land of Oz was a strange place, which grew stranger with every passing second.

It was hours later when they finally stopped. It could have been days for all Alice knew. The dark, cloud covered sky gave no indication as to the passage of time. Never before had she been so desperate to catch a glimpse of the sun. Or the moon, for she was not particular.

They had entered the forest Glinda had mentioned shortly before they stopped for their break. The layer of trees blocking the sky did nothing to improve her disposition. The farther they traveled into the gloomy interior of the country, Alice found her mood deteriorated more and more. Whether it was from the harshness of the environment or her continued lack of sleep, she could not be sure, nor did it matter much to her. In her foul mood, she did not care about anything, except resting.

When they finally did stop, she threw herself to the ground at the base of a tree. Her hands massaged the aching muscles in her legs, but that only seemed to make the pain worse. Never before had she walked for such a long period of time. When walking around Oxford, she was accustomed to being able to take frequent breaks on a park bench or the like whenever she had become too tired. She had never had such an ache before. Once she had sat down on the ground, she couldn't possibly imagine getting back up.

Strangely enough though, her feet didn't hurt at all. Even after all the walking, that was not where the worst of her pain came from. Whatever magic her shoes had somehow protected her feet from aching. If they only had the ability to do the same for the rest of her body.

"We do not have much time to rest. It is important that we make as much progress as possible. The cabin is not far from here. We should reach it by midday tomorrow." Glinda remained standing, staring into the depths of the forest as if she could see all the way to its center. Even with the tired lines etched into her face, she looked unwilling to stand still for a single moment longer than necessary.

"No." The word was out of her mouth before Alice had

even realized it had formed in her head. Intentional or not, there was no point in stopping. "I'm sorry, Glinda. I understand that this is important, but I can't go on for another second." She didn't try to hide her exhaustion. If anyone were to look at her face, they would see it plainly written there.

"I know you're tired, Alice, but we really must push on. Our time is getting shorter and shorter. We must act with the utmost speed."

"But how am I supposed to defeat the Witch if I am dead tired? I can't keep going at this pace."

"Alice is right, Glinda. You cannot keep pushing her like this." Scarecrow had taken a seat against a tree opposite of Alice. It didn't seem possible, but even he looked worn down. He had definitely lost a good bit of his stuffing and really could use a bit of straw to replace it. Unfortunately, the forest floor did not appear to have any to spare. "And the same goes for you. There is no way that you will be able to keep this up for much longer. Even you have your limits."

Glinda continued to stare deep into the trees, but she was thinking over Scarecrow's words. For a second, Alice was sure the woman would ignore them and insist they start moving immediately. Instead, her shoulders slumped in resignation. "We will rest here for the night."

[93]

Alice let out a very audible sigh of relief. Her head fell back until it rested on the hard trunk of the tree. It did not make for a very comfortable pillow, but Alice would take it. Her eyes began to fall under the heaviest weight she could ever remember.

"But we must…"

The rest of Glinda's words were lost to her for she had already fallen fast asleep. For once, she hoped her dreams would be about home instead of other worlds.

Chapter 7

She woke with a start. Hours must have passed as she slept. What little she could see through the trees showed that the blanket of clouds had finally moved on, leaving a dark sky dotted with stars. It was the first time that she had seen the sky since she first got there. She was a little surprised to find that it was so similar to the one over Oxford. In Wonderland, the sky was filled with hundreds of different shades of color, even at night. Maybe it meant that there was a closer connection to Oz and her world than she knew.

Looking around the small area where they had stopped, she found Scarecrow curled into an extremely tight ball that would have been uncomfortable for anyone with bones. He appeared to be asleep, but did a scarecrow actually need sleep? He was as far from the dying embers of the fire they had built as he could possibly be. That was probably the wisest idea. The last thing they needed was a member of their own party bursting into flames.

Glinda, though, was nowhere to be seen. Alice looked, trying to peer into the darkness of the trees. Maybe the woman had gone into the forest to have privacy while she slept. But with the darkness as complete as it was, she couldn't make anything out. For a second, Alice considered the possibility that something had captured Glinda and taken her away. She quickly dismissed the idea though. As much as she said her powers were "diminished", Glinda was more than capable of taking care of herself.

That left only one alternative. Glinda had walked off into the trees while they were sleeping. Had she left for good? Had she decided to go on to the cabin alone? Or was she perhaps just taking a small break from them and had planned to be back before anyone had awakened. That was certainly possible. Alice had planned to sleep for several more hours.

As for what shook her from her sleep, Alice searched for that too. She did not have to look for long before she had her answer though. A loud squawk came from the trees over her head. Immediately, she was on her feet, trying to find the source of the hideous noise. She found it in the lowest branch of the tree that she had, moments before, been sleeping against.

It was a crow, but unlike any she had ever seen before. Its all black feathers were shiny with a thick ooze that coated its entire body. When it opened its mouth to screech again, Alice could make out small, sharp teeth in its beak. But the worst part of the bird had to be its eyes. They looked almost human as they turned to stare straight at her. It was what Alice imagined a crow's nightmare would look like.

Her first instinct was to reach out and call to the bird. Her father had once bought her a canary who liked to fly out of his cage and land on Alice's finger. She would stroke the thing's head while it made the most adorable chirping noises. The hideous crow would probably not do the same.

Her second thought was to run, but she couldn't see that going any better for her. The bird was much bigger than the ordinary crows that Alice had seen in the past. If she tried to escape, surely the beast would be on her before she had made a few steps. Perhaps if she stood perfectly still, the thing would grow tired and fly off to haunt some other unfortunate person.

As if in answer to her thoughts, the bird spread its wings, revealing their large span. She had no idea that crows could grow to such proportions. It must have been some kind of magical creature because, between its size and appearance, it was not possible for it to be just an ordinary bird.

It opened its beak and released a loud and horrifying screech. The hellish sound was enough to make Alice forget herself and run in the opposite direction. But she couldn't. She tried to move, but her feet were planted firmly on the ground.

[97]

No, not her feet. Her shoes. They held to the dirt as if they were connected. Her feet twisted inside them, but she could not force them free.

The evil looking crow chose that moment to take flight. It flew straight at Alice's head. And still the shoes would not release their hold. She raised her hands to cover her face and ducked, hoping that the bird might miss her, but knew the hope was most likely futile. Her hair blew in the wind created by the beast's wings as it flew past her head. The brush of oily feathers made her skin crawl.

When no bite or scratch came, she chanced a peek between her fingers. The bird had moved away, heading into the tangle of branches over her head. Its caws grew more and more distant. She watched as the bird disappeared into the dark leaves.

Once the beast was completely out of sight, the shoes let go of their grip on the ground. Alice nearly stumbled into the dirt as she was suddenly released. Why had the shoes been so insistent that she stand still? Did Glinda know they had the power to do that? And if she did, why hadn't she bothered to tell her?

Once her heart stopped pounding in her chest, she looked around their makeshift camp. Scarecrow was still curled up against the tree, not having moved an inch.

[98]

"What good is a scarecrow if it just lets crows attack when you're sleeping?" When there was still no response, Alice let out a disgusted breath and turned away from him.

The fright she had received left her with shaking hands and a dry mouth. Sleep had come so quickly that she didn't stop to think about asking Glinda where she would find water, which she desperately needed. Glinda wasn't there to ask and she was quite angry with Scarecrow, so she was left with only one alternative. She would have to search for some herself and hope it was not too far. After what had just happened, she didn't think it wise to venture into the forest on her own, but her need was just too great.

Carefully, she stepped into the trees. With no clue which way would lead to water, she chose a direction at random. As soon as she passed the tree line, the small amount of light from the dying fire was lost. The flames were so weak they could not penetrate the thick darkness of the forest.

Mostly using her hands and feet to guide her, she made her way through wide tree trunks and twisted roots. With nearly every step, she had to regain her balance or risk falling face first onto the dirt. The small heels of the jeweled shoes did not help her with walking. Alice felt a small hatred for the shoes.

It didn't take long for her to get utterly lost. Even if she knew where water was, would she be able to see it in the inky blackness? The same went for finding her way back to where Scarecrow slept. She could call for help, but what were the chances that he would hear her when he hadn't stirred an inch throughout the entire crow attack? And who knew where Glinda might be?

She continued to stumble through the trees, cursing her stupidity. What had possessed her to walk into dark, unfamiliar woods all alone? Her heart began to pound in her chest again. Would she be stuck until there was some light in the sky to see by? Who knew how long that could be? The blanket of dark clouds could be back any moment, blocking the little light that could make its way through. Alice knew she could be lost for a very long time.

But she wasn't. Her foot caught on a gnarled root and she stumbled. But instead of hitting pitch black dirt, she found herself rolling over soft grass, free of the trees and the oppressive darkness they offered. A large moon hung in the sky, illuminating the land in a soft white glow. How could the moon be out, but no light made it through the trees? Alice reasoned that the forest must have a powerful enchantment on it causing it to be shrouded.

Walking away from the ominous trees, she took in her new surroundings. She was in a small stretch of land. Though it wasn't a lush clearing, the grass still looked more alive than anything Alice had yet to see in Oz. On one side, stood the tree line that lead back into the shadowy forest, which she was not eager to reenter. On the other side was a vast chasm that was easily a mile wide. It went on, seemingly forever, in both directions until it reached the dark horizon. It was almost as if some great power took the ground and broke it in two so completely that it reached all the way to the core of the land. The chasm was so deep that Alice couldn't make out its bottom.

There was nowhere for Alice to go but back. Even if she could cross the massive canyon, it was going in the wrong direction. If only she had thought to bring a torch from the campfire with her. She shouldn't have been so careless, but the incident with the crow had rattled her deeply.

She had just sat down on the ground, deciding to rest for a short time, when she heard it. The sound of a twig snapping, like it had been stepped on, coming from just inside the tree line. She looked over the area, but could not see anything. Not that she thought she would, with whatever spell caused complete blackness to fall over the trees.

She held her breath, silencing the only sound in the clearing. In the eerie quiet, Alice felt a cold that reached down inside. She felt a shiver crawl up her legs and suddenly wished that Glinda had made her dress just a bit longer.

Another sound reached her ears. At first, it was so faint that she could barely make it out, but slowly it grew louder and more distinct. There could be no mistaking it, a low animal growl coming from the edge of the forest. The only comparison Alice could make to it was the sound that her cat, Dinah, made when she'd hunt mice in the attic, only much deeper. It was a dangerous sound.

She couldn't move from where she stood, but it had nothing to do with the shoes. In fact, she felt a strong desire to run, but her legs would not obey. Fear had her rooted to the spot. Why had Glinda chosen to venture into a forest that was obviously filled with dangerous creatures and then abandon her to them?

Something shifted at the tree line, very close to where Alice had come from. Slowly, a paw moved into the light, followed by a fur covered leg. Her eyes grew wider and more alarmed. The paw alone was twice the size of her head. As more of the animal came into view, Alice began to feel sick to her stomach.

It was so much more than an animal. It was a beast in every sense of the word. Dirty, brown fur covered its entire body, matted in places with something darker that Alice was positive she didn't want to know the identity of. She had seen pictures of bears in her books, so she knew that's what the creature's body was. But never before had she seen a massive bear with a tiger's head on its shoulders. The beast's mouth dripped a thick, white foam on the ground and its own fur. She could smell the foul order that clung to its breath. It took a great deal of effort to hold back a gag. It would not be prudent to offend the creature, if it could be offended in the first place.

She locked eyes with the animal. For a second, she hoped that it was like the tiger she saw in the council meeting and possess humanlike qualities. But that hope was quickly dashed when it opened its mouth to reveal razor sharp fangs as big as Alice's hand. It let out a feral growl that made her body shake uncontrollably.

Why couldn't she move her legs?

The beast lunged. It moved at an incredible speed, considering its size. Alice screamed out, but was still unable to run. Even if she could, was there any escape from such an animal? Surely, it would catch her no matter how quick she was. Wasn't it better to just accept her fate? She closed her eyes and waited for the beast's attack.

But it never came. Instead, she was startled by the loud roar of pain it gave off. She opened her eyes again to find it falling to its side. It howled to the night sky, pain flashing in its eyes. Despite what it was about to do to her, she felt sorry for the creature. It was only doing what its instincts demanded. If it had any sense, Alice was sure it would not be attacking people in the forest. She reached out her hand to offer the dying beast what little sympathy she could.

The axe slamming into its head made her jump back. Blood flew from the wound, splattering everywhere, including Alice. Spots of dark red stained the pristine fabric of her dress. She was spared of getting any on her face but she still felt the turn in her stomach as if she might vomit.

She looked incredulously at the axe sticking out of the animal's skull. Following the handle up, she saw that it was in the grip of a strong pair of hands. Muscular arms pulled the weapon free with a disgusting squelch. Alice looked higher to find silver eyes staring at her with revulsion.

"Brax?"

Chapter 8

"Are you insane?" Brax pulled a cloth from his back pocket and began to wipe the blood and other matter from the blade of his axe. "Walking through The Dead Woods in the middle of the night is about as stupid as you can get. It's an invitation for a Kalidah to eat you. You're lucky the trees themselves didn't grab you, what without a fire to keep them off." When his blade was clean, he looked at the cloth before discarding it in the grass.

Alice could not speak. Her mind was having trouble catching up through her state of shock. She had never witnessed anything die before in her life, not even the mice that Dinah caught. But right in front of her eyes, Brax had slayed a living thing in the cruelest way imaginable. Her clothes were covered in the result of that action.

Brax continued to stare. When she gave no response, his expression changed from distaste to questioning. "Have you gone mute? Or are you just as simple as the Council believes you to be?"

The insulting question jarred Alice from her stunned

silence. "Did you have to be so brutal about it?" She looked down and examined the blood that stained her dress. "I almost believe you enjoyed it."

"Most people would say thank you when their lives have just been saved."

"But it was a simple beast. It was only following its instincts. Could you have not thought of a more humane way to dispatch of it?"

Brax crossed his arms. His lips twisted into a smirk that irritated Alice to her very core. "Should I have invited it to a tea party? Tried to mend our differences through civilized conversation? That may work in the places that you've been, but not in Oz. Not anymore."

"I suppose you think that is a valid excuse for such brutality."

He stepped closer to her. "That thing would have killed you in seconds and eaten your bones. The Kalidah is Oz's most dangerous predator. And that was even before the Witch brought on the Dark Era. There is no reasoning with them."

With him so close, Alice tried to ignore the oddly appealing scent he gave off. It confused her and threatened to dampen her irritation. She would not forget what he had just done. "Perhaps the reason they are so vicious is because the barbaric way the people of Oz slaughter them."

He stepped away, turning his head. Inspecting the Kalidah's dead body gave him an excuse not to meet her eyes. "Maybe I was wrong to stand for you in the Council meeting. Glinda may have been wrong after all. If this is enough to unnerve you, how will you ever be able to do what needs to be done?"

Alice opened her mouth to ask exactly what that was, but she was interrupted by another rustling in the trees. She straightened up and locked her eyes on the jostling branches. Brax moved to stand in front of her, axe raised, ready for an attack. She wanted to put her hand on his shoulder to stop any rash action on his part, but her fear had returned and she found herself unsure. Was Brax right about the creatures?

But her fears were needless. It was not another Kalidah coming to devour her. It was Glinda, wide eyes searching frantically. When she spotted Alice, her whole body relaxed in relief. "I could not find you at our camp. Then I heard screaming." She put her hands on Alice's arms, squeezing tighter than necessary. "Is everything okay?" She turned slightly, noticing for the first time that Alice wasn't alone. "Brax, what are you doing here?"

As soon as Glinda began speaking to him, Brax's demeanor changed. His axe lowered and his spine straightened.

"I have been following you since you left Gillikin territory. I wanted to ensure your safety since the Council seemed unwilling to do even that. It is a good thing I did because Alice," he paused at her name, barely containing his disdain, "decided to go wandering in the night and was nearly mauled by a Kalidah."

Glinda looked aghast at the news. Her face grew ashen at the sight of the dead body on the ground. "Alice, you mustn't go wandering off like that. These woods are a very dangerous place, especially at night. Much worse could have happened to you."

Instead of feeling the shame or horror that Glinda expected, she became angry. "And how was I to know that? You gave me no warning about what I would find in the trees. How am I to know anything when you won't tell me? You brought me to this land full of horrors and have left me ignorant to its dangers." Her voice rose, echoing in the night.

Glinda looked ashamed of herself as her eyes darted back and forth from Brax to Alice. "You're right. I have withheld information from you, but only so…"

"And where were you anyway?" Alice shouted, cutting off whatever explanation Glinda was about to give. "What was so important that you would abandon us in a forest where even the trees are vicious?"

[108]

Brax backed away, scandalized. "You should not speak to Glinda that way. She deserves..."

"It's okay, Brax." Glinda put a soft hand on his shoulder. "If anyone has earned the right to speak in such a manner, it is Alice. She has been most patient in a situation she did not ask to be a part of." She turned to Alice. "I am sorry for leaving you at the camp. I never dreamed that you would wake and go wandering on your own. If I had, I would not have left."

"Where did you go?"

"My magic is diminishing. There is a ritual that I can do that strengthens me for a short time, but to perform it I must be in complete isolation. The woods are ideal for it because the animals that live here will not try to harm me. It was worth the risk of leaving you unattended, for we are going to need me at full strength for the things that we might face."

Alice was silent, but not appeased. She was struck again by the feeling that there was more to Glinda than she was aware. For someone known as the Good Witch, she kept a great many secrets. Far more than she should when other people were affected. What else was she not telling Alice?

"We should not stay here." Brax stepped up again. His eyes scanned the clearing, on alert for any possible attack that may arise. "There may be more Kalidahs in the area. We cannot depend on Glinda's protection to keep us all safe."

"Yes, I agree. Come, Alice, we must get back to camp. If Scarecrow has awakened, then he will be quite worried."

Alice followed them, but only because she had no other choice. She was not at all inclined to go anywhere with either one of them, but her only other option was to stay in the clearing and wait for another beast to attack. Taking a deep breath, she plunged back into the overwhelming darkness of the trees.

Chapter 9

Sleep did not come easy for any of them for the rest of the night, except for Scarecrow, who had not awoken once. Even when they returned to the camp, he didn't stir. Alice was jealous of his obliviousness.

At the first sign of light, the enchantment causing total darkness having broken with the dawn, the party set off. Brax kept close to Alice as they walked through the trees, but did not look particularly pleased about it. The surly look on his face did not make Alice any more eager to have him near, especially with his axe hanging at his side.

Through the hours of restlessness during the night, Alice had a lot of time to think. Yes, Brax had clearly saved her life. If he hadn't acted, there was no telling what horrific things that beast would have done. He had no choice, but to kill it. It was the manner in which it was done that gave her pause. She was not comfortable with the swift ferocity of it. It reminded her a little too much of Wonderland's Queen of Hearts ordering the removal of so many heads.

Their trip through the forest was a quiet one. Mostly.

Scarecrow rattled on about topics that no one was very much interested in and too unaware to realize that no one was listening to him. Normally, Alice would at least attempt to be polite, but she was too busy searching the woods for any sign of danger. Once or twice, she could swear a tree's branches moved toward her only to find nothing when she turned to it.

"The trees are not as agitated during the day. The worst they might do is throw an apple or two our way." Brax didn't look at her when he spoke, continuing to stare at the path ahead.

Alice didn't acknowledge that she had heard him. She did not trust herself to be able to see past her anger and be civil. In her mind, it was best to stay quiet and follow the rest, though on the lookout for flying apples.

As far as she could tell, they reached the small cabin around midday. The ever present clouds had finally gone, allowing small rays of weak sunlight to work their way through the forest canopy. Even then, it was hard to tell the passage of time, being so deep in the trees.

Alice was amazed at what a small amount of light could do. With it breaking somewhat through the leaves, she could almost see the former beauty of the place. If only it was enough to make her forget what a dangerous place she was walking through. She was reminded of that fact strongly when they reached their destination.

It was a cottage in name only, and just barely at that. The extreme decay of it made Alice question the safety of walking inside. The building looked like a strong breeze would easily collapse it. She was not anxious to be inside if that were to happen.

Unfortunately, Glinda seemed to have no issue with stepping inside. Alice watched as her blue dressed disappeared behind the rickety walls. Brax was quick to follow in her footsteps. Only the Scarecrow lagged behind. After many false starts towards the entrance, he finally slumped his shoulders in defeat and walked to meet Alice.

"It seems I should have asked the Wizard for some courage as well."

"Being smart enough not to walk into a remarkably dangerous situation requires its own kind of courage."

Scarecrow brightened at the idea. Alice could see the great pride he took in the use of his brains, but something nagged at her. If the Wizard was the great "humbug" that Glinda said, was he able to give Scarecrow any brains in the first place? Or were his brains part of whatever magic that could bring a straw man to life?

"I do wish I could be more like Brax though. He's so

quick to jump into action. It's the kind of bravery Oz needs during these times."

Alice managed to hide the fact that she rolled her eyes at his comment. She failed to see anything spectacular about Brax, other than perhaps his hypnotic eyes. And maybe that lovely scent he had about him. And that maybe we was rather attractive, in an obvious sort of way. But everything else about him seemed utterly ordinary, if not downright irritating. She crossed her arms, having no desire to speak of him further.

"You shouldn't be so hard on him, Alice." Scarecrow responded to her outraged face with a raised hand. "You don't hide your emotions as well as you think. I can see the way you are when he is near. I don't know what happened in the forest between you two, but you should give him a chance. He has not had it easy."

Alice's expression softened. "What has happened to him?"

"In the years before the Witch came to power, Brax's family had become very prominent in Munchkin Country. They were once simple farmers, but after the Fall of the Wicked, there was talk of electing Brax's father to the Council. He refused, of course, but was still held in high regard by many of the citizens. When the Witch launched her first attack on the East, his entire family was killed. He escaped, but was left an orphan. If he hadn't been found and taken in by Jantik, he might not be alive today."

"Who is Jantik?"

"You saw him in the Council meeting. He was sitting next to Brax in the audience?"

"The tiger?" Alice asked, incredulously. "That explains so much about him. He was raised by wild animals." Alice had never met someone who gave truth to the old expression.

Scarecrow's cloth face stretched until it looked strange and elongated. "Alice, I would not let Brax hear you speak like that. He is very protective of Jantik and does not take kindly to anyone referring to him as wild."

For a second, she was about to argue her point, but stopped. If Scarecrow was being truthful, then that tiger, Jantik, was Brax's family, the only one he had left. It felt inappropriate to speak ill of that. Instead of continuing, she turned a little to face the shack, her small sign of surrender.

"Nick would be heartbroken to see what has come of his home."

Alice wasn't sure who he was talking about, but grateful for the subject change. "Nick?"

"Nick Chopper, the Tin Woodman. Long ago, before we met Dorothy, this was where he lived. It had been in his family for many generations. He took great pride in this land, even after the Wicked Witch of the East set him up to be made of tin. That is until he got caught in the rain and rusted. It wasn't far from here that Dorothy and I..."

From inside, Glinda's voice rang out, bringing Scarecrow to a stop. "Alice, please come in here."

Alice really did not want to walk inside. She had a feeling the second she did the roof would come falling down on her. There did not seem to be anything, but magic, holding it up. But she knew that Glinda would not give her a choice in the matter. Carefully, she started towards the doorway. Sensing her hesitation, Scarecrow joined her, placing a soft hand on her arm. They would be brave together.

The interior of the cabin did not look any better than the exterior. The floorboards were rotted in some places so badly that Alice could see dirt below. Dust and grime coated the walls. Bits of furniture lay strewn across the floor. From the smell, she knew that it was occasionally lived in by animals who did not concern themselves with hygiene. Alice had to choke back a gag.

Glinda was in the corner, bent over a particularly large hole in the floor. Brax stood guard behind her. Alice moved closer to them, her shoes thudding against the old wood. As she stepped deeper into the room, the smell grew more foul. She desperately wanted to run back outside where the air wasn't quite so suffocating.

"Look at this, dear."

Alice looked in the hole and found something that did not remotely belong there. Sitting in the dirt was a shining object that sparkled even in the dim light of the room. It was circular in the middle with brilliant arms branching in every direction. Not only was it made from fine silver, but its surface was imbedded with hundreds of tiny diamonds each shone with their own light. Even sitting in a hole of dirt, the thing was unspoiled. A brilliant snowflake that could easily fit in the palm of her hand.

"I can't remove it. I believe that it is waiting for you." Glinda's voice came out in an awed whisper. Her eyes were transfixed on the sight. "Reach in and try to take it."

Alice was hesitant, but she tried anyway. The sooner she did, the sooner that she would be able to leave the deplorable shack and the whole forest behind. What had Brax called them? The Dead Woods? The name, along with everything else about the place, felt sinister beyond anything she had ever experienced before. She would be glad to be done with it.

Her fingers grazed the dirt as she reached in. Carefully,

she took the thing in her hand and lifted it from the hole. It was cool to the touch, cooler than Alice imagined it would be. After all, it had been sitting in the ground for longer than she knew. But to feel it, she would have thought it had been laying outside on a pleasant day. Alice stood, still staring at the glittering jewel. "It's most peculiar."

The light from the diamonds and silver pulsed as if it had a heartbeat. It grew more intense with each throb, until it filled the whole room. It was so bright that she reached up to cover her eyes from the glare before realizing that she didn't need to. It didn't hurt. She stared into the light with amazement. A small smile spread on her face.

It wasn't until the light started to grow dimmer that she realized she had been holding a deep breath. She released it and watched as the light grew weaker and weaker. After a few seconds, the jewel returned back to its glittering self.

"Have you ever seen it do that before?" Brax whispered. Alice was thankful that he kept his voice low. If had spoken any louder it would have disturbed whatever presence had just been there. Maybe he wasn't such a clod after all.

"It has done that once before. Years ago, just after Dorothy entered my castle."

"Does it react to people from the Other Land?" Scarecrow slowly reached out to touch the shining jewel, but stopped before making physical contact. His hand hung in the air for a second before he pulled it away.

"I believe it is reacting to the shoes, just like it did with Dorothy. It never behaved this way in the presence of the Wizard." Glinda took it from Alice. Once free from the ground, it didn't have a problem being handled by others. "It's just further proof that the relics want to be together."

Alice started to ask a question, but was cut off by the unnaturally loud call of a bird. Her blood froze at the sound. It was the same as the one she heard the night before coming from the grotesque crow that attacked her. Had the bird been following her the whole time? Why? What could it possibly want from her?

All the color drained from Glinda's face. Quickly, she placed the jewel in a bag that Brax handed her. Pulling the strap over her head, she positioned it to where it hung across her chest. Alice had to confess that the contrast between the rustic bag and her regal dress was off putting. "We must leave at once." There was a franticness to her voice, one that set Alice even further on edge.

Brax lead them out of the rickety shack. They did not make it far. Alice bumped into Glinda's back as Scarecrow stumbled into hers. She was irritated until she saw the reason

Brax had stopped dead in his tracks. The sight was the only thing that could make her want to run back into the little house that she hated so much.

The same crow sat on a branch right in front of the door. It's dark, almost human eyes, stared straight at them. It tracked every small movement they made. It hopped lower and lower on the branch, moving ever closer. Then, it opened its beak wide and released another nightmarish screech. Alice had to cover her ears from the shrill sound.

"Let's make our move now. I can stop it if it comes at us." Brax took a step forward, but Glinda caught his arm before he could take another.

"It's too late for that. The crow is not what we should be concerned with."

Something large rustled in the trees in front of them. Alice's heart stopped as the branches all around started to move. "What is it?"

Her answer came in the form of a creature stepping from the shadows of the trees. It wasn't a Kalidah, though she almost wished it had been. It was so much worse. Standing on two legs and reaching nearly twice Alice's height, its whole body was covered in short, grayish fur. Patches were stained with a dark brown substance that she hoped was dirt, but somehow knew wasn't. It was a horrible approximation of a monkey, evidenced further when it unfolded a set of wings from its back and stretched them to their fullest span. Feathers, the same color as its fur, fluttered with the movement.

From the trees, more of the winged monkeys emerged until they were completely surrounded in a circle of fur and wings. They all had a similar appearance, including the feral look on their faces. A couple even had strands of drool hanging from their mouths. Alice did not like the implications of that.

The first one to step out of the trees moved forward, taking on the role of leader. When it opened its mouth to speak, small jagged teeth were exposed. They could easily tear flesh apart. Did everything in Oz have fangs?

"You know why we are here." Its voice was deep and guttural, making his words difficult to understand. "We do not wish to harm you, Mistress Glinda, as we have served you loyally in the past. Just give us the girl as our new mistress demands."

Glinda, despite her obvious fear, stood tall. "I cannot allow you to take her. If not for the influence of the helmet, you would see that it would be wrong. If you wish me no harm, then you will go no further on your mission."

"We have no choice. We are bound to our mistress. As you once controlled us, you know that. The helmet is now gone, but the magic remains in our mistress. We serve her for all time."

Glinda took a step closer to the lead winged monkey. It was only because Alice stared so intensely that she was able to see the slight shaking in Glinda's hands. "I also know that you were free once. And you can be free again. But not if the Dark Era is allowed to continue."

"Who rules Oz is no concern of ours. We only follow the will of the holder of the helmet. Now allow us to complete our assignment."

The monkey made a sudden movement towards Alice but was stopped by a violent burst of energy that radiated from Glinda herself. Alice felt the wave of energy as it passed through her and moved beyond. Without having to be told, she knew that it was the feeling of magic. She began to have a sense of the power that the land possessed.

The monkey was frozen where it stood. If it was possible it looked even more vicious. Turning, she saw that it was the same with all the monkeys. Wings spread and claws outstretched, they stood as if they were hideous statues.

Glinda spun on her feet. "We must go. The binding spell will not hold them for long. Their magic is powerful and cannot be easily contained." Glinda's terror did not ease Alice's nerves about the situation any. "Which way do we go, Alice?"

"Me?" she asked, eyes wide. "How am I to know? This is your land?"

"Trust the shoes. Let their magic guide you."

The shoes? Alice was being asked to put her faith in a pair of shoes? How could Glinda ask that of her? Yes, she was told they were magic, but what proof did she have of that? And with zero experience wielding magic herself, how was she supposed to make the shoes do anything?

But, on the other hand, the shoes had shown signs of having a will of their own. When the crow had flown at her, the shoes had not allowed her to run away. They planted themselves firmly on the ground and no amount of force could free them. Why was that? Because they knew the bird was no real danger at the moment and running would only have made the situation worse?

"Please, hurry, Alice." Glinda was beginning to grow hysterical, a sight that was both frightening and unnatural.

Alice moved to take a step in the complete opposite direction of the lead monkey. As her foot moved back to the ground, she felt the smallest pull from the shoe. It lead to the right, back towards the cabin. Taking another step, she felt the same pull leading her towards the back. There were fewer monkeys there and it would be easier to slip through their line.

[123]

Already, the strange creatures' faces were starting to slowly twist in anger, the binding spell wearing off.

'How curious?' With each step she took, the pull became less and less. It only returned when she tried to take a step off the path that she was headed. She did not linger on the strangeness of being led by her own shoes, there was no time for that. Only a short distance from the cabin and they could hear the howls of the monkeys in the air. It would not take them long to be overtaken.

They quickened their pace through the trees. Scarecrow was having trouble navigating the branches and brambles without getting snagged. One particularly nasty cluster snared him in multiple places and stopped him completely. Brax ran back for him, examining the damage. Alice wanted to help as well, but Glinda would not allow it, pushing her onward.

"I'm sorry about this." She heard Brax's words seconds before he took both hands and ripped Scarecrow free of the confining branches. The sound of tearing cloth made her catch her breath. But Scarecrow did not show any pain despite large patches of his "skin" being missing. From the newly made holes in his body, bits of straw fell to the ground. Clumsy hands attempted to hold as much of it in as possible, but he would not be able to run and keep himself together at the same time. Brax solved the problem by picking up Scarecrow and cradling him in his arms. The straw man must not have weighed a great deal because Brax was able to continue running like he wasn't carrying anything in his arms.

Crashing came from behind them. She didn't need the screeching to know that the horrible monkeys were close. They had gained on them quickly. Alice did not see how they were going to make their escape, which would have made their flight pointless.

Just as she was ready to give up all hope, the shoes gave a jerking pull to the left, so strong that Alice almost fell to the ground. With effort, she kept her balance and followed where the shoes directed her. Did they know some way out that no one else did? She doubted it because, from all she could tell, they were leading her to a giant tree covered in a deep red moss. Sure enough, when she reached the trunk of the tree, the shoes refused to allow her to walk around it.

"What now? Do we climb it?"

Glinda stepped around her and put her hands on the spongy moss, feeling it all over. "This is perfect. No, there's no need to climb. This offers a much better form of escape."

Underneath her hands, the moss start to glow and crawl like it had been granted life. It parted, revealing a large opening in the tree, which was hollow and could easily accommodate all of them. But would it be an effective hiding place? Alice couldn't make out anything in the depths of the tree.

Brax did not hesitate, climbing into the unknown interior of the tree with Scarecrow in his arms. As soon as they had disappeared inside, Glinda waved a hand in the direction in which they had come. A strong wind blew through the area, eliminating all traces of the straw that had come from Scarecrow, inadvertently marking a trail to their location.

"In you go, dear."

Alice paused only for a split second before leaping into the darkness. Nothing in the tree could be worse than what was chasing them. Glinda followed right behind her. The second her hand was removed, the moss began to grow back quickly, covering the entrance. It also blocked out all traces of light, leaving them in total darkness.

Safe inside, they could hear the scream of a very angry monkey, muffled by the solid wall of moss.

Chapter 10

The tree turned out to be much more than a mere hiding place. The darkness concealed stairs dug into the hard dirt. After Glinda lit a fire at the end of a stick, which set Scarecrow into a fit of worried mumbling, Alice could see the stairs led to a hollowed out tunnel that stretched further than she could make out. While it didn't look particularly inviting, it was still a better alternative than what waited outside.

"We must get to the other end of this tunnel and then somewhere safe as quickly as we can. The Witch has spies everywhere. Your arrival did not go as unnoticed as I had hoped."

They started down the tunnel, its narrow walls forcing them to move in a single file line. The walk went by silently, no one having much to say, not even Scarecrow. It was just as well because Alice didn't feel like talking to any of them.

She knew she had made a promise to Glinda and the Council, but she was having serious doubts. It had not been her wisest decision to agree to such a task without it being clear exactly how dangerous it would be. But Alice found it unfair that Glinda put her in such a position without the decency of a warning. Her apologies were always followed by an even more dangerous obstacle to overcome. No wonder the Council found her ridiculous. She was in no way up to the job that Glinda asked of her. And all the talk of Dorothy wouldn't change that.

But how was she going to remove herself from the situation? She had no idea how to get back to Oxford, but she suspected that it couldn't be done without Glinda's magic. If that was the case, then Alice was completely at the Good Witch's mercy. Would Glinda withhold that power to force Alice to continue?

At some point, the tunnel had grown even darker. The light from the torch was no longer a match for the looming blackness ahead. It felt like they had been walking for hours, but again without clues as to the passage of time, there was no way to be sure. It was only the ache in Alice's legs, but not her feet thanks to the shoes, that told her they had been moving for so long. And unfortunately, since the tunnel had become so narrow, there was not enough room to take even a small rest.

Alice could have soldiered through, if it had not been for the ceiling slowly sloping downward, making the tunnel even more compact and harder to navigate. She was reminded of the time when she was foolish enough to eat a Wonderlandian mushroom and grew to several times her normal size. But it was even worse because of the very real chance of a collapse. The idea of being trapped underground made her chest hurt. She felt her feet quickening their pace, even though it was hardly possible in the confined space.

Sweat began to fall from her forehead, stinging her eyes. Her hands moved across the claustrophobic walls. From what she could tell, the others were not having as hard a time of it. But why should they? Scarecrow didn't have bones or muscles that could ache, while Glinda and Brax were probably used to traveling in such a manner. Just something else that Alice could add to the list of things she was unprepared for.

She nearly cried out loud when, after what had to be hours, the tunnel began to move upward. It had to be a sign that they were reaching the end and would soon be aboveground again. Sure enough, a short time later, Glinda called for them to stop. They had come to a solid wall, a dead end. In the dim light of the torch, Alice could see that the wall was made of the same red moss that had been on the tree. And like before, Glinda placed her hands on it. The red glow began to fill the tunnel.

Alice quickly wished to return to the darkness. In the harsh light, she could make out things that had been embedded in the dirt walls that she had been touching. Small bones protruded from the hard packed earth. Littered throughout the tunnel were skeletons of creatures that Alice could not identify. She got the feeling that even if she had studied those types of subjects back home, she would still not be able to pinpoint their origin. They came in various sizes, ranging from as small as a rodent to as large as a person. Her stomach gave a great heave at the thought.

As soon as the wall parted a fraction, the tunnel flooded with a fresh breeze, replacing the stale air they had been breathing. Alice could wait no longer and began to forcibly free herself, which included pushing Scarecrow out of her way. Luckily, Glinda had already climbed out or she would have been bowled over by a straw man practically taking flight. The moment that Alice was clear of the opening, she vomited on the grass.

When there was nothing left to purge, she gulped air into her lungs over and over until her head began to spin. She could not stop the tears falling from her eyes. It wasn't until a soft hand fell on her back that she began to regain her composure.

"Traveling underground can be rough. I threw up my first time as well." Brax's voice was different from all the other times he had spoken to her. It was softer and not filled with the meanness that she had become accustomed to. When she looked up into his eyes, she saw pity had replaced the customary contempt. "Do you feel better now?"

She nodded her head. Her breathing had begun to slow and was more manageable. Her stomach had calmed, which was good because she needed to keep what little was in her stomach for energy.

"Good." He stood straight again. His eyes returned to their former hardness, though perhaps a little less sharp. "We must continue. The monkeys might be aware of where the tunnel lets out and could be on their way here now."

Alice clumsily got to her feet. The heels of her shoes were unsteady as she fought to regain her balance. "He could have at least helped me to my feet. That would have been the gentlemanly thing to do." But Alice was only talking to herself, for the rest of them had continued on without her. With little choice otherwise, she followed.

It only took a few minutes to clear the area of sparse trees in which they had emerged. They stood at the edge of the downward slope of a very large hill. At its base sat a small cluster of oddly shaped buildings. From the placement of the domed shaped structures around a central point, Alice thought it must be a village or a town of some sort. Though it looked rather out of place, considering the terrain she had seen so far.

Glinda had only paused long enough for Alice to catch up before starting down the hill. "The town of Gale. We will be able to get a hot meal and maybe a couple hours of rest."

"Gale? As in..." Alice struggled to keep pace with Glinda. Her legs still felt weak from the tunnel.

"Dorothy Gale," Brax answered. He turned his head slightly to look at Alice. "Many of the Munchkin towns changed their names after the Fall of the Wicked. Most were named in tribute to Dorothy for all that she had done."

Alice wanted to ask for more in way of an explanation, but it was clear there would be no more conversation. So, instead, she turned her attention to making it down the hill.

But getting down was harder than she anticipated. Mostly because she had to stop quite often to help Scarecrow to his feet, who was having more trouble than normal maintaining his balance. Finally, since the other two took little notice, Alice let him lean against her as they walked. She could see the large amount of straw he had lost in their flight. There were places on his body that felt almost empty.

"Will you be okay?"

"Yes." He was weak and could barely speak. Alice assumed he was going through the same thing as a regular person bleeding to death. "I just need to visit a barn when we arrive in Gale. Surely, they will have some straw to spare."

Alice hoped that was true. Scarecrow was not in good shape. She wondered what would happen if he lost all of his straw. Would he die? Is that how it worked for straw men? Or would he still live, but just as an empty sack of cloth? Alice did not know and did not want to find out.

Just like when they came out of the tunnel, Brax and Glinda continued walking when they reached the bottom of the hill. They showed little concern for Alice and Scarecrow, who struggled behind them. This angered Alice, but she was becoming accustomed to their rude manners. Her mother always told her not to judge people based on their rude moments for they could just be having a rough day. That was a lesson that she was trying very hard to remember, but without much success.

"You would think they wouldn't be so eager to leave us behind? Do they even remember that we are here?" Her voice strained with the effort she was putting forth to drag Scarecrow, whose legs had all but given out on him.

"It's easy to forget your manners in the Dark Era. The past years have not been easy for them, Glinda especially. She has had to take on so much since the arrival of the Witch. Many citizens of Oz have turned against her and blame her for not stopping the horrors we have endured. That has changed her

[133]

from the woman that she once was. She has become determined and will stop at nothing to achieve her goal."

Alice knew that was true and that 'stopping at nothing' included withholding certain information. Not only that, but she couldn't help the nagging sensation that Glinda was lying to her. About what she did not know and dreaded the moment she would find out.

"It will be alright, Alice. I promise." Scarecrow made an attempt at a reassuring pat on her shoulder, but he didn't have the strength in his hand.

She flashed him the best smile she could manage and hoped he didn't notice that it did not reach her eyes.

As they got closer to Gale, people started to gather in their doorways. They were all small of stature. Alice was finally getting to see the Munchkins that she had heard mentioned. They weren't the cheerful people she envisioned from the word munchkin. Like everything else in the land, they had a worn down and dirty look to them. Shoeless children huddled at their parents' feet.

As the group made their way down the dirt road, eyes watched them. The rumble of voices broke the silence that had fallen over the air. Alice could hear the occasional whispered word.

"Glinda."

"Stranger."

"Witch."

Alice could not tell from their tone if they were meant to be insulting or hopeful. She had seen different reactions to Glinda, mostly in the Council meeting, so she didn't know if the Munchkins were on her side or not. Perhaps walking straight into their town was not the smartest course of action.

Glinda didn't take notice of the stares and whispers. She walked with her head held high until reaching the center of the town. In the middle of a small dirt courtyard, a tree was on a slow journey into decay. Bare, thin branches drooped low to the ground. It matched the despair Alice had witnessed. Surrounding the tree was a short wall made of crumbling stone. Glinda stepped up onto the wall and turned to face the town.

"People of Gale! We need your assistance!" Her voice echoed, able to be heard all over the town. "Please, come out!"

Slowly, more Munchkins appeared. They came from doorways and alleys to make their way to the small courtyard. They formed a circle around Alice and the others. Cautious eyes looked up at Glinda, but as Alice looked around, she saw that many were looking at her instead. Some of the smaller children, being Munchkins who barely came above her knees, tried to inch closer to her to get a better look. It made her very uncomfortable because she feared they might try to attack her.

"We will not ask much of you." Glinda looked out over the crowd, flashing them a warm look. The harshness Alice had seen earlier was gone. "We only need a place to sleep, a meal, and some straw for my friend."

At the mention of straw, many of the Munchkins turned their attention to Scarecrow. Small rumblings passed through the crowd. Their proximity and numbers amplified their high squeaky voices. Alice could only make out a word here and there, but she did recognize the name Dorothy more than a few times. Children reached out to touch the loose cloth of Scarecrow's body before being quickly pulled back by their parents.

One of the Munchkins, slightly taller than the rest of them, pushed his way through the gathering. He wasn't rude about it, but forceful. The others quickly parted so he had adequate room, clearly of some importance. "Glinda," he called out before even reaching the front, "you should not have come here. And you should not have brought her." He pointed a finger directly at Alice. "You are only making us targets for the Witch's wrath."

Glinda turned to the man, but showed no change in her serene expression on her. "But, Triff, you are already a target and have yet to do anything to deserve it. You are the mayor of this town, surely you can see that. As for Alice, she is only here to help us in our darkest time."

The crowd began to rumble again. It wasn't exactly clear what had set them off. The mention of the Witch? Alice's presence? Their normal fears? But whatever it was that upset them, it worked very well. The people were getting angrier and angrier.

Glinda raised her arms in an attempt to calm the restless crowd, but to little effect. A couple of the Munchkins picked up their children and ran to their houses, completely ignoring Glinda. Those who stayed did not look pleased. Alice searched for a way out, but couldn't see one. It seemed that everywhere she went, she ran into another obstacle.

"We can't take the risk. Harboring you could cause the Witch to attack us. We have been lucky so far and can't allow you to put us in that danger."

The Munchkins began screaming out in earnest. Insults and demands for them to leave rang through the air.

But Glinda was unconcerned. With her hands still held out towards the hostile crowd, she tilted her head. "I tried to do this the nice way." The calm, warm look melted from her face. A flash of light burst forth from her hands and Alice was temporarily blinded from the brightness.

When she opened her eyes again, she saw that all of the Munchkins in the courtyard were still as statues, just like the winged monkeys had been. Alice walked through the frozen Munchkins, amazed and rather terrified.

"Why must everyone in Oz be so difficult? You would think they'd realize that I'm only trying to help them?" Glinda stepped down from the wall and meandered through the crowd. Giving each a disappointed glance, she waved a hand in front of their faces as she passed. Briefly, a pink glow surrounded each Munchkin. "You will help us. You will provide us a place to sleep and a warm meal. Your farmers will tend to Scarecrow and stuff him with the best straw available. This is your duty as citizens of Oz."

Alice watched wide-eyed as Glinda worked her way through the entire crowd. What was she doing to them? Had she used magic to hypnotize the entire town? Alice had difficulty believing it was possible. It certainly wasn't moral. How could anyone who called themselves a "good witch" be comfortable with stripping people of their free will?

The pink auras faded, leaving the Munchkins with vacant eyes. "We will help." A chorus of emotionless voices echoed in the courtyard. "It is our duty."

An unnatural smile formed on Glinda's lips. It unnerved Alice. After what she's done, the last thing Glinda should be doing was smiling. For the first time, Alice felt like she was in the presence of a real witch.

"Now, that's better." Glinda clapped her hands together twice and walked away, followed by a mass of Munchkins.

Chapter 11

The meal was awkward. They were served in the room that had been found for them. Some Munchkin family had been forced to give up their house for the night so they could have a place to sleep. Alice would have been fine with a small corner of a barn somewhere, especially after seeing the family they had displaced. She could see the displeasure in their eyes, but because of the spell, they had no choice. The same was true for the people who brought them food. The spell could only force them do it, not make them happy about it.

And Alice couldn't blame them. She was disgusted by the Munchkins' fate. She thought she was there to help the people of Oz, not to turn them into slaves. How could Glinda believe she was helping these people? More importantly, how could she do such a thing to her own people, who looked to her in their time of need?

Scarecrow had been gone since the Munchkins had taken him away. Alice hoped that he was being taken good care of in the barn. She also hoped he would return quickly. Tensions were very high in the little room that passed for a Munchkin house.

Brax had fallen asleep almost immediately after eating. He sat on a bed, his head pressed into a corner of the wall, lightly snoring. Glinda sat in a chair by the door, deep in thought. Alice couldn't bring herself to look at the woman without feeling nauseous. She wished, more than anything, she could leave the room and walk all the way back to Oxford. But that wasn't an option, not after seeing Glinda's show of power.

"You should sleep. We have a long trip to the Emerald City. You will need your rest."

Alice didn't respond. The only sign that she had even heard Glinda's words was her crawling under the blanket and finally closing her eyes.

The bed was too small. It was probably the perfect size for a Munchkin, but Alice had to bend her legs to fit. Even with the cramps, it was still more comfortable than sleeping in the Dead Woods. She tried her best to enjoy the feeling of laying on a mattress, not sure when she might have another opportunity.

Pushing thoughts of Glinda from her mind, Alice drifted off to sleep.

If only her rest would have lasted.

The sound of movement woke her. She didn't know how long she had slept, but the sky outside was dark with night. It was hard for her to make out the room around her. Afraid of what might be there, she tried to keep still while her eyes adjusted to the dark.

It was only Brax moving about the room. Alice couldn't see clearly, but she could tell from the familiar axe at his side. He was searching the floor for something. He kept his movements slow, apparently to minimize the noise he made, but it was no use. 'The lumbering oaf doesn't know how to move quietly!'

Alice was about to ask why he was lurking about in the dark, but he suddenly stood up, finding whatever he was looking for. He stuffed an old folded up slip of paper in his pocket and was out the door before Alice could form the words to stop him.

'Where could he possibly be going at this time of night?'

Before she even realized she was doing it, her feet were moving. She didn't spare a thought to the fact that, even though she was in a bed, she still wore the jeweled shoes, something that would usually have struck her as odd. But she was too focused on following Brax to concern herself.

The night air felt almost pleasant. In the sky, a large moon shone brightly, giving off enough light that Alice could see with ease. The streets of the little town were empty. The silence that had descended gave the whole place an uncomfortable feeling. Alice almost turned back, but then she caught a slight movement down road. She was never one to deny her curiosity.

As she began to follow Brax down the dirt road, he turned a corner without realizing she was there. Her feet began to move faster. If she lost him, then leaving would have been for nothing.

But she hadn't need to worry. As soon as she turned the corner, a little faster than she should have perhaps, she slammed into the solid form of Brax standing there. The impact knocked Alice from her feet and onto the dirt. From the ground, she looked up at Brax who had his arms crossed over his chest.

"Go. Back." His words were harsh and final. The look in his eyes was angry, not quite to their previous level of contempt, but angry all the same.

She stood quickly, dusting off her skirt. "No." She met his eyes with her own anger. "I am going wherever you are."

"You are not. Alice, this is none of your concern. Go back to bed."

"I am tired of you people telling me what to do. You and Glinda have been ordering me around since I was brought here. How can you expect me to help you when this is the way I'm treated?" Her voice began to rise, breaking the oppressive silence of the night.

"Alice..."

"No!" She waved her hand in front of him. It had been an effective gesture when people used it against her. "I did not ask to be brought here, Brax. You say you need me. Glinda says I'm the key to saving Oz. But you leave me in the dark and keep your little secrets. I'm finished. Start telling me everything or I will leave. I'm sure this Witch I'm always hearing about will be happy to send me home just to get me out of Oz." She hadn't even been thinking such a thing before. The threat just flew out of her mouth, but once it had, it seemed like an obvious solution. But would she be any safer asking for help from the Witch than she would be from Glinda?

They continued to stare each other down for a full minute, neither of them blinking. Brax, tried to use the few inches he had on Alice to intimidate her. But she was having none of it. Her anger was an equal match to his height.

Finally, after several tense moments, Brax relented. Shifting his feet, he was unable to meet her gaze any longer. "Fine. You may come." He turned and began walking away, not waiting for her to follow. Calling over his shoulder, he added, "No talking."

It was Brax's only rule and the one that Alice would never be able to follow. Jogging lightly to catch up, she spoke. "Where are we going?"

Brax didn't answer, instead growling in frustration. His

pace quickened. The stomp of his boots thudded against the hard ground. But Alice would not be deterred. It was almost as if she could not help herself.

"It's just rather suspicious to be sneaking out in the middle of the night, don't you think? If it was something truly important, why couldn't you tell everyone? Why wait until everyone else had gone to sleep? It makes you look as if you have something to hide."

That was when Brax made his biggest mistake of the night. "It's an errand of a personal nature. I would have been back before anyone woke in the morning." While he saw the matter as closed, Alice took his responding as a signal to keep going.

And she did. Their walk through the night was littered with a barrage of questions. They started out merely about the "personal errand" they were on, but quickly evolved into various topics. Mostly she seemed obsessed with finding out about his life in Oz. Had he always been a fighter? How had he come to know Glinda? What did he like, when not roaming the land?

With each question, Brax became more and more irritated. His fists clenched tighter and tighter until his knuckles shone white. Each step he took was harder than the last until he had fallen into a rhythm of stomping. He had not given her any further answers, but still she persisted in her questioning. He was trying incredibly hard to keep his temper under control, but she was not making that an easy task.

The night grew darker as they came upon a small cluster of trees. Alice followed as Brax led her near them, but not inside. They walked along the edge, Brax releasing his frustration by kicking various bits of debris out of his way.

Alice reached down and picked up something off the ground. Even in the moonlight, the apple shone a vibrant red. She rolled it in her hands, surprised to find that it was still firm and not at all rotting like she would have expected. Until she held the apple, she hadn't realized how hungry she was. Even though she had eaten only hours before, it felt like forever since her last meal.

She brought the apple to her mouth and was moments from biting into it when Brax slapped it from her hands, sending it back to the ground.

Alice gaped at him, completely affronted. "Why did you do that? Have you always been this rude or is this something that you have reserved for me?"

"In the name of Lurline, Alice, have you always been this curious? I don't know how things worked in this Wonderland of yours, but it is different here. You can't walk around without the smallest bit of caution." With a swift kick, he sent the offending fruit back into the trees.

"It was only an apple, Brax. What harm could it have possibly done?"

"The Fighting Trees are among the oldest living things in Oz. The land's magic has been flowing through them for years. Since the Dark Era began, the magic seeping into their roots has turned the trees from merely unpleasant to incredibly poisonous. They throw the apples in hopes that a gullible traveler will eat them. One bite will put you into a coma that you will not wake from."

Alice looked appropriately chastised. Perhaps it would be better if she showed a little more restraint in her curiosity, no matter how difficult that would be. Since she was a child, she had become accustomed to letting her imagination run wild. It was very different in Wonderland, where there were certainly dangers, but nothing like what she saw in Oz. Wonderland may not have been the world of benign frivolity that Dodgson made it out to be, but at least there was never any danger from her eating a simple apple. The Land of Oz was not a place that Alice would have ever chosen to visit. When she did find a way back to Oxford, she hoped to never see it again in her lifetime.

Instead of continuing her questions, of which she still

had a great deal, she fell into step with Brax, who had slowed his pace some. She tucked her hands under her arms in an effort to resist the urge to touch anything else that she might come across.

"I'm sorry, Alice. I don't mean to be so harsh." He still did not look in her direction, which she was grateful for, so he would not see how shaken she truly was. "Life in Oz has been hard for a very long time. It is easy to forget that not everyone knows of its dangers. I am merely trying to protect you."

She had the urge to tell him that was a very good reason for him to be more understanding, but she didn't. What would that accomplish? Besides, she could try to be more understanding towards him as well. He had been forced to live in the nightmare that was Oz far longer than her. That was bound to have an effect on anyone. He had also had saved her life twice.

As her own way of appeasing him, Alice remained silent for the remainder of the walk. Even when she thought she saw a tree branch move in the dark as if to grab them, she held her tongue. When it didn't come too close, she chose to believe it was only the breeze or a trick of the moonlight causing her to see things.

Whatever it was, Alice felt a huge sense of relief the moment they had cleared the cluster of trees. But, in Oz, you

[148]

couldn't leave one horror behind without stumbling on another. What lay before her made tears well up in her eyes.

Debris lay scattered as far as she could see. Small, shredded scraps of wood littered the ground, mixed with long rotten crops. It wasn't just the destruction that pulled at Alice's heart. She had seen enough of that in Oz. It was the obvious violence behind it. The farm, for that's what it had to have once been, wasn't just torn apart, it was decimated.

Brax stopped at a pile of wood that looked as if it would crumble at the slightest touch. Not far from where he stopped stood two blackened polls stuck in the ground. She could only assume that it must have been all that was left of the farm house, the original home of the shreds of wood.

"What happened here?" Her own words choked her as they came out.

"What else?" Brax sounded different, darker and more dangerous. "The Witch. She came through here with a vengeance. Her forces didn't do this. She took it upon herself to wreak havoc here. And it was brutal."

He began walking into the field of debris, carefully pushing the ruins out of his way with his foot. He stopped near one of the blackened poles. Squatting down, he dug through the pile of filth that had built up at its base. As he swept away years' worth of rotted vegetation, a small, flattened stone came into view.

"Boq. In loving memory." She read the words on the stone, aware that she sounded unnatural in the silence that had fallen over them. "Who was he?"

Brax continued cleaning off the stone with a care that Alice didn't believe him capable. He meticulously made sure every bit of it was free of dirt. "My father."

Alice faltered for a response. What could she say? Nothing would express the sympathy she wanted to convey adequately. Regret suddenly filled her for forcing him to bring her along. She wished she had left him undisturbed. If she had known how deeply personal his errand was, then she would never have left her bed.

"He met Dorothy, you know?" He spoke in barely a whisper. Alice had to kneel in the dirt next to him so she could hear. "She stayed the night on her way through this area. I was only an infant at the time. My mother says she even played with me some. That's why, after the Fall of the Wicked, my father became so well respected. His small connection to Dorothy made the people turn to him when it came time to set up a new government. There was even a movement for him to become the new leader, but he would have none of it. He said that he would always be a farmer, no matter what life sent his way. He took such pride in this land. My brothers, sister, and I spent hours listening to him teach us how to care for it." He pushed the last bit of detritus from the stone and sat back on his feet. "That was until the Witch. My entire family died in the fire she started. But it wasn't enough to just get rid of someone the Munchkins turned to for guidance. She had to annihilate everything we worked our whole lives to build. I think she took pleasure in it."

"I'm so sorry, Brax." It felt insufficient, but what else could she offer? Her hand softly landed on his knee.

"She destroyed so much of Oz, but this was one of the first. And definitely one of the most brutal."

"Is that why you started fighting? Because of the deaths of your family?" Alice tried to catch Brax's eye, but he would not look away from the grave marker in front of him. "Because you were angry?"

He stood abruptly, knocking her hand away. "Of course, I'm angry. Wouldn't you be? I survived her attack. I was left an orphan at an age when I needed my family the most. If it weren't for Jantik's kindness, I would have died not long after my family. The least I can do, since I am able, is to make the Witch pay for this, and every other atrocity she has committed. Why do you think I hunted down Glinda in the first place? I thought she would..."

He was cut off as a massive body barreled into him, throwing him a good distance. Alice's scream filled the empty night. Taking a couple steps back, she instinctively put space between herself and Brax's attacker. It was only then that she could take in its matted fur and folded wings.

A flying monkey had tracked them down at last.

Chapter 12

The monkey let out an ear piercing shriek as it pinned Brax's arms to the ground. Flecks of spittle flew from its fang filled mouth. Brax tried his best to keep the monster at bay, but he was slowly losing the battle. Alice watched his arms bend with a sense of dread. It would only be a moment before the horrific beast had him.

"Alice...run." Brax strained to speak through his clenched teeth.

It was then that Alice made an unexpected choice. Her feet were moving before she even realized what they were doing, but not away from the attack. She worked hard to keep her mind empty, not to think about what she was doing. If she did, she feared she would turn in the other direction. And that was not an option.

The impact was like crashing into a brick wall. Her entire body was jarred as her shoulder slammed into the beast. She struggled to breathe as all the air rushed from her lungs. But she didn't stop, refused to stop, not until she was sure that Brax wouldn't be hurt by the monkey.

Luckily, and quite surprisingly, her plan worked. The massive animal was thrown across the ground. Unfortunately, Brax was not released from its grip. He was launched into the air with the momentum. A clanging sound echoed around them as the weapons hanging from his belt came loose and scattered.

It took Alice a moment to recover herself. The world tilted in an odd manner. As her breathing began to return to normal, the slight wave of nausea passed. Her vision cleared just in time to see the monkey climbing back on top of Brax, more ferocious than before. Sweat beaded on Brax's forehead as he used all his strength to keep from getting bitten.

"Alice....go...Glinda..."

She knew that if she left, there would be no way that he would survive. That he had lasted as long as he had was a miracle in and of itself. She could not abandon him, even if staying might mean her own death as well. There was a very good chance that running would lead her to the same fate. The monkey could outrace her, even if she could make her way back to Gale without Brax.

Looking around for something, anything, that would help, Alice spotted the scattered weapons. Some of them she hadn't noticed much before when Brax was carrying them, but there was one she knew well. The large axe that he favored lay not far from her, just a couple of feet, the light of the moon reflected on its steel blade.

Again, without waiting for her thoughts to catch up, she grasped the handle of the axe. The wood was smooth in her hands. Obviously Brax had gone through great care to keep his weapon in the best condition. It felt heavier than she thought it would be. Having never had the need to carry such a thing, she wasn't sure exactly what to expect. Would she have the strength required to wield it?

The monkey was so preoccupied with trying to rip Brax to shreds that it paid no attention to what Alice was doing. It was relatively easy for her to get the jump on it. The axe raised high over her head, she came up behind them as they rolled on the ground. As swiftly as she could, she swung the weapon, bringing it down with as much force as she could muster. The strike was only effectual in that it knocked the monkey slightly off balance, but not enough to stop the attack completely. It also had the undesired effect of making the monkey turn its attention to Alice at last.

For a brief moment, she could see the tinge of madness behind its feral eyes. The beast released another howl that shook Alice. A wave of hot, foul breath smacked her in the face, bringing tears to her eyes.

She only had a second to react. Any hesitation would

give the monkey time to strike back, making all her efforts worthless. With every bit of strength in her arms, she swung the axe again. She let out a sound she never thought she could make, a scream that would have sounded more natural coming from a wild animal.

The blade struck home. Her hit couldn't have been better if she had been aiming. The sharp edge of the blade pierced the monkey's head, silencing the beast immediately, its face frozen in a scream that no longer sounded. Alice, shocked, let go of the handle, hands covering her mouth. Without her holding on for support, the dead body slowly sank to the ground, the axe still protruding from its head.

Alice couldn't move. A tremor ran through her body, the full gravity of what she had done hitting her. She stared at the small pool of blood beginning to form around her feet. It took her a second to realize that there were tears streaming down her cheeks. There was nothing she could do about them but let them fall.

Brax painfully got to his feet and made his way over to her. Tentatively, he reached a hand out, but stopped a couple of inches from actually making contact. "Alice..."

"I...I...I didn't..."

Quickly, Brax pulled her in and wrapped his arms tightly around her. One hand landed in her hair and stroked it soothingly. "You didn't have any choice, Alice."

His words did nothing to calm her. She had taken the life of another living thing for the first time, in any world. She had always been so careful not to harm anything living before, not even the smallest bug. But she had violently killed an obviously intelligent creature.

"He would have killed me. And, after that, you. It was the only thing you could do."

She buried her head in his shoulder. Her answer was muffled by his shirt. "I've never..."

"I know. I had the same reaction my first time. Taking a life is never easy. But sometimes it's necessary for survival."

She wanted to say that it wasn't a good enough excuse, but she couldn't. Deep down inside, she knew he was right. What other way out was there? The monkey would have killed her for sure. And then the whole mission to save Oz would have been ruined. She only wished that could make her feel better about it.

He began to pull away from her, but kept one hand on her arm. The other hand pulled at a strand of her hair, pushing it back from her face. "Thank you, Alice. You saved my life. You were very brave."

Her eyes met his. It felt like she was seeing him for the

first time. Or, more accurately, that he was letting her see him. The strong, angry exterior had melted away, leaving a young man with a hopeful expression. Alice had to wonder if he would look like that all the time if the past years of misery hadn't befallen the Land of Oz. It was a small glimpse at an alternate reality.

Alice should have stepped back then, but she couldn't seem to break the connection that had formed. Brax seemed unable to move away as well. His fingers continued to fiddle with her hair. Alice couldn't figure out what his next move would be. Was he going to lean in and kiss her? Was that what she wanted?

She never found out because they nearly jumped out of their skin at the sound of a heavy pounding on the ground. Something large was coming in their direction. Alice mentally shook off any reservations she had about what she had done and prepared for the possibility of having to do it again. She braced herself for the appearance of another winged monkey.

In the light of the moon, she could see an indistinct shape moving towards them very quickly. As it got closer, she could tell that whatever it was ran on four legs. That meant it had to be some sort of animal. Another monkey? A Kalidah? Something worse? She felt Brax's body tense next to her as he waited.

But as the creature got even closer, Brax visibly relaxed. Did that mean that he knew what it was? Were they not in danger after all? She couldn't make herself let her guard down until she knew for sure, not with everything she had seen in Oz.

It wasn't until it was almost upon them that Alice could see decently in the moonlight. Its color was distorted in the pale illumination, but she could see enough to know that she recognized the animal as well. It was not likely she would forget the giant tiger sitting in the council hall. She released the breath that she had been holding.

"Brax!" The tiger called out in a gruff voice. Even though she knew it could talk, had seen Brax have a whispered conversation with it, and was not the first talking animal she had met, it still threw her off to hear such a human voice coming out of its mouth.

The tiger skidded to a stop just feet from where they stood, showering them with loose dirt. Judging from its heavy breathing, she guessed that it had been running hard for some time. A look of relief washed over the animal's face when it finally stopped.

"Jantik, what are you doing here? You're supposed to be guarding the Council."

Jantik fought for breath before it was able to answer.

[159]

"The Council sent me to find you. I knew you would be near this area and assumed you could not resist coming here."

"Why? What could be so important that they would leave themselves unprotected?"

Jantik stood on its hind legs, towering over both Alice and Brax. "The Council has fled. They are hiding in a small Gillikinisian town, one of the safe places we set up long ago. They are being protected by as many soldiers as we can spare. It was our only option."

"Why are they in hiding?" It was Alice who spoke up. What could have changed so drastically in the time since she was last there? What would make the Council run from their hall, especially Syrdip, who surely would have refused to move just to make life more difficult for others?

"The Witch has begun laying siege to large parts of Gillikin and Munchkin Countries, worse than ever before. Her Winkie army is destroying anything they cross." Jantik cast a glance at the body of the monkey laying on the ground, the axe sticking from its head. "You have managed to escape all attempts she has made to capture you, so now she is moving through the land, searching for information as to your whereabouts."

Brax shifted. His spine straight, he was tenser than ever before and on full alert. Any pleasure he had from seeing Jantik immediately vanished. "We don't have much time. We have to go."

He said this to Alice as if there were a possible chance that she would argue. But she knew that if the Witch was anywhere near, then they had to move quickly. She gave a quick nod of her head to show that she understood.

Brax turned back to Jantik. "Get to Gale. You'll be able to get there much faster than we would. Inform Glinda and Scarecrow of what has happened. Tell them to meet us at the Fighting Trees, using whatever magic is needed."

Jantik nodded, acknowledging Brax's orders. "I can be there in less than an hour. Keep yourselves safe until then. The Witch's army could arrive at any time."

"We will." Before Jantik could lower all four legs to the ground, Brax took a step forward. "Thank you."

The animal closed the distance between them. Its massive paws wrapped around Brax. Ordinarily, it would have looked like the tiger might be trying to maul him. But she could see the tenderness in the embrace. She also heard the deeper meaning in Brax's thank you. It gave the impression that it might be the last one between them.

And just like that, with a roar, Jantik leapt away from them and began running at full speed again in the direction that

[161]

Alice and Brax had come from. They watched until the trees in the distance blocked their view.

They were once again left in the silence of the night.

"What now?" Alice whispered, the very air itself feeling fragile.

"We wait for Glinda and Scarecrow." Brax stared off in the direction that Jantik had run, as if trying to catch one last glimpse. "And then, when they get here, we make best possible speed for the Emerald City."

Chapter 13

The name Emerald City gave Alice a certain expectation of what she would find when they got there. The reality was nowhere near the image she had in her mind. The first thing she thought upon hearing the word 'emerald' was that the city would be mostly, if not completely, green. But as they walked through the streets, there was no green to be found, not even a blade of grass.

She walked up to a building that was covered in several layers of what Alice could only hope was dirt and grime and began wiping it off. It took some force because the dirt must have been there for a great deal of time. Underneath, there was nothing but a dull, brownish colored wall that also failed to meet Alice's expectations.

The Emerald City was not what Alice thought a city to be. She could tell that at one time it was, but no longer. The tall buildings that reached for the cloud covered sky were in extreme states of disrepair, some missing large chunks of their exterior. It didn't take long to find where most of those missing sections had ended up. The streets were a maze of bricks, stone, wood, and other materials. Several large piles of debris had no doubt once been entire buildings that could no longer stand.

And, most of all, it was completely deserted.

They had arrived earlier in the morning, Glinda expending some of her precious magic to produce a bubble to travel. In the time that they had explored, Alice had not seen another person, not even an animal, talking or otherwise. The emptiness made Alice more uneasy than the demolished buildings and the rubble filled streets. The city was large enough to fit many people in it, more than even London maybe, but it was devoid of life.

"The evacuation of the Emerald City did not go as planned." Scarecrow was talking again, but no one was paying attention. Their eyes were locked on the crumbling city around them, taking it all in. Even Glinda and Brax, who must have seen it before, could not look away. "We lost many citizens in the mayhem. The attack came without warning. Before the Witch struck the city, no one even knew there was trouble forming in Oz. We were all unaware of the danger we were in."

Alice let Scarecrow's lecture drone on until she was hardly conscious of it anymore. Part of her was too caught up in the sights, and the other part just couldn't listen anymore. How many stories would she be forced to hear about destruction?

How many horrible things would she have to listen to before it was too much? The scraps of farmland did not prepare her for seeing an entire city in ruins. She could not begin to imagine the loss of life that had occurred in such a place.

As if to emphasize the heartache of the scene, Alice kicked over a rock to find a torn and tattered doll beneath it. She bent down to pick it up. It was crudely made, obviously stitched by hand. Even though it was crooked and uneven, Alice could tell that it was supposed to resemble a little girl. The fabric of its dress was faded and worn, but the blue and white checkered pattern could still be seen. Turning her eyes away, she let the doll fall back to the ground and wiped away tears.

She carefully stepped around tall piles of stone to make her way over to Glinda, who had not spoken a word since they had arrived in the city. It was hard to read what the woman might have been thinking because her facial expressions changed from one second to the next. Despair to rage to regret in the blink of an eye. Alice was hesitant to intrude on Glinda's self-imposed silence out of fear that she might trigger an angry reaction. The last thing she needed was another stern lecture, not after the one she got for "wandering off in the middle of the night like a foolish child" earlier in the morning. Glinda was sounding a little too much like her own mother for Alice's comfort.

"What have we come here for? It doesn't appear as if the Witch has left any part of this city untouched. She must have found whatever it is we are looking for?"

"The Witch may have ransacked the city, but even she does not know all of its hiding places. There is a relic here, in a place so secret that only a select few knew of its location. Legend tells that this relic was destroyed hundreds of years ago, but that was only a ruse to keep people from searching it out. Not even the Council knows that it still exists."

Alice wasn't surprised to learn of another secret that Glinda was hiding. Sometimes, it seemed like all that the woman did was hide the truth. Alice really had to question if Glinda should hold the title of Good Witch. Her actions did not fit.

"And where is this relic hidden?"

"The Wizard's Palace. That is our destination."

Glinda tore her gaze from the wreckage around them and began walking. Once they had made their way through the piles of rocks and other debris, Alice could see that the road was still made from yellow bricks. Though it was in better shape than other stretches of road that they had come across, it was still in serious disrepair. Alice wished that she had been able to see it in its full glory. All of Oz had the potential to be so

[166]

beautiful, she could tell, if the land wasn't covered in a nightmare version of itself.

Scarecrow fell in step beside her, more sure-footed after the people of Gale had stuffed him and patched his body. He continued his running commentary on the once magnificent city and all the damage done to it, but Alice couldn't even hear his voice. She had never met a person like Scarecrow, though she was still not sure if he counted as a person, who could test the limits of her boundless curiosity. She had to spare a moment to wonder what her mother would have to say about that.

It didn't take long to get to what Alice assumed was the Wizard's Palace. Even with the severe damage done to it, the building still towered over the rest of city. It was clear that this Wizard had tried to impress everyone with the grandeur of the place, perhaps to hide the fact the he had no real power. And the citizens of Oz obviously swallowed the lie.

The entrance to the palace was a set of massive double doors made of stone. Even through the thick layer of dust, the doors had a greenish tint to them, maybe emeralds had been used in the construction after all. But in front of the doors stood a mountain of large boulders and wall fragments that reached at least halfway up them.

"This may be problematic." Glinda eyed the stones as if they had done something to personally offend her. "My magic won't be of much use here. When the Wizard renovated this place, he was mindful to use magic resistant materials for the outer walls, a safeguard against the Wicked Witches."

Without the use of magic, Alice did not see a way of getting through. Some of the smaller fragments could be moved by hand, but the majority of them were easily two or three times her size. She would never be able to move them. Perhaps they could climb, but there was no telling if they would be able to open the massive doors from that height. And the pile did not look very stable.

Brax, however, would not be intimidated by the unmoving rocks. He walked right up to them and began pulling the smaller ones away. Angry grunts issued from him as he launched the rocks away from the rest. He was making good progress, separating some of the more daunting obstacles with ease, until he reached a long, smooth boulder that must have been heavier than it looked. His fingers couldn't find a sufficient grip on its edge as he tried to force it from its position. Determined, he refused to abandon the futile task. Sweat began to pour down his forehead and the muscles in his arms bulged at the effort. Finally, his fingers lost the fight and he went flying to the ground. He let out a groan as he sat up.

Glinda merely stood off to the side, shaking her head slightly. Then she walked up to the base of the large pile. Her eyes contemplated the sight in front of her. Her fingers played with a long strand of her hair.

"Is there another way in?" Alice called out.

"Oh my, no. The Wizard was extremely paranoid. The few secret tunnels the designers had been able to sneak in were sealed by hand a long time ago. He could not risk anyone discovering his secrets."

"But..."

Whatever Alice was about to say died in her throat. Her attention was drawn to a rock that had fallen off the pile and rolled to the ground all on its own. She was about to say something completely different when another one dislodged from the rubble with such force that it landed at her feet.

Glinda began to slowly back away, so completely self-absorbed that she didn't even notice when she came an inch from stepping on Alice's foot, not that Alice would have even noticed herself.

Slowly more stones and boulders began to fall. It was not only the smaller ones, but the boulders as well. The smooth rock that Brax had tried so desperately to move began to crack along its surface. A muted thud sounded as more cracks started

[169]

to form. Beneath her feet, Alice could feel the ground rumble with each thud. Instinctively, she tried to back farther away, but again her shoes would not let her move. She was rooted to the spot.

As the thuds became louder and more intense, it became more obvious that something was pounding into the rocks from the other side. Something was trying to get out of the obstructed doors. Alice couldn't help but wonder if that something was friendly or, as was her experience, dangerous.

She did not have long to find out. The pounding became more frequent and violent, causing even larger rocks to tumble to the ground and the boulders to crack deeper. Finally, in a shower of dirt and rock, the pile exploded outward. All four of them covered their faces to protect against the cascade of debris. Alice, maybe unwisely, risked a peek through her fingers just in time to see a building column, like those she had seen at her father's school, flying through the air. It sliced through the air above her head and crashed into the building across the street.

Looking back at the doors, which were wide open, she found a woman standing there. She was taller than the Munchkins that she had come across, but not very tall by normal standards. The woman seemed out of place amid the crumbling ruins. Her white dress was pristine with an apron tied

[170]

around her slender waist. The only bit of color on her attire was an intertwined O and Z stitched in green across the front of her apron. Her hair was pulled into a tight, neat bun that was pinned to the back of her head. She looked at the group, expectantly.

Glinda straightened up from her crouched position and saw the woman. Her face melted into disbelief. "Jellia?"

At the sound of what must have been her name, the woman flew down the steps, dodging the rubble with ease. She ran with her hands outstretched towards them. Reaching Glinda, both women immediately took each other's hands. "I knew you would come. I have been waiting for such a long time, but I knew it was not in vain."

Glinda still stared at the woman in openmouthed shock. "Jellia? What are you doing here? The whole city has been abandoned for ages. Why didn't you leave with everyone else?" She pulled the smaller woman into her arms and hugged her tightly.

"And go where? The Emerald City has been my home for longer than most people have been alive. I've lived here since I left Gillikin Country as a young girl. I would never abandon the city, no matter what befalls it."

Alice was a little taken aback by the woman's tone.

Standing amidst the rubble, she spoke with pride, like she didn't see it as the crumbling mess that it was, but the glittering city that it had obviously been. Alice was impressed with Jellia's ability to ignore the shambles her world had become.

"Besides, I couldn't leave." Her voice dropped to barely a whisper. "You know I couldn't. There would be no one left to guard the palace."

As if suddenly reminded they were not alone, Glinda turned to the others, her arm wrapped around the other woman's shoulder. She waved her free hand at her three companions. "Jellia, you know the Scarecrow. This is Brax. And this," her voice taking on more serious air, "is Alice. She is from the Other Land. She has come to help us."

Jellia moved out of Glinda's arm and approached the others. "Jellia Jamb, at your service." She held the edges of her skirt and gave them a polite curtsy. "Welcome to the Wizard's Palace. What's left of it, anyway."

A smile beamed from Glinda's face, one that wasn't forced or fake or unnatural. The appearance of Jellia had transformed her. She was not only beaming, but looked positively hopeful, something that Alice had never seen. "Jellia is a trusted friend and loyal Oz citizen."

Jellia's face reddened in embarrassment. "You flatter me, Glinda. I am merely a maid who has been around since the days of King Pastorius. Just because I have outlasted the king, the Wizard, the Scarecrow, the Council, and now the Witch, I don't know if that qualifies me as trusted and loyal."

Alice stared hard at Jellia. From her words, it sounded like she was several years old, having worked in the palace for a long time. But she did not look much older than Alice herself. She couldn't see how that was remotely possible, but then again, she was in Oz.

"You are too humble. A mere maid would never have been entrusted with the secrets you have been. It's a great responsibility." Glinda placed her arm around Jellia once more. "And speaking of, that is why we have come."

Jellia looked around at the assembled group, nodding. "I assumed as much." She neatly turned on the heel of her flat shoe and began walking towards the doors of the palace. There was no indication, but it was implied that they were to follow.

Chapter 14

The inside of the palace was by far the most curious sight that Alice had come across. Quite simply, it did not belong. Every inch of the place practically sparkled with newness. The floors shined emerald green. In the highly polished surface, Alice could see a clear reflection, like she was walking on a green tinted mirror. Walls and statues gleamed in the light of hundreds of candles. It was the first place that she had seen in Oz that was whole and unblemished.

Jellia, noticing Alice's astonishment, moved to walk next to her. "I've been alone for a very long time, ever since the evacuation. The palace did not fare well in the attack, as I'm sure you can tell from the outside. I've tried to restore it as best I could."

"You've done an amazing job. This place looks like nothing happened to it at all."

"Well, I am a maid. A good one, if I might say." Jellia's lips spread into a proud smile. "I haven't been able to add much to the fight against the Witch's tyranny. This is just my small way of not letting her win."

Alice continued to walk in step with Jellia, following her

from the entrance hall to a side room that led to a tightly spiraling staircase. Because of the space, she reached out her hand and touched the wall for balance. It felt smooth under her fingertips, smoother than any stone she had ever felt. Something about the touch of it made her smile, taking small comfort in the fact that something so nice could still exist in the world. A quick look behind her found Brax doing the same thing. For just a moment, their eyes met and he gave her a small nod.

The palace turned out to be a maze of corridors and staircases. It felt like they had been walking for miles, slowly climbing higher and higher, but never getting anywhere. For most of the walk, Glinda and Jellia chatted happily in hushed, girlish whispers. Their attitude completely changed the atmosphere around them, no longer quite as dire as it had felt. Alice was trying to enjoy the small reprieve from the seriousness of their mission.

When they had climbed what had to be their hundredth set of stairs, Jellia led them into a room that rivaled the entrance hall in size, if not surpassed it. It was a tall room, reaching several stories high, with a domed ceiling. The room itself was relatively bare, consisting of a smattering of stone benches, most surrounding a large, golden statue placed in the exact center of the room. Throughout the outer edges of the room were a series of pedestals, each containing a different object encased in glass. One of the pedestals was empty and surrounded by broken shards. On the far side of the room were a pair of doors that reached halfway up the wall.

"What is this place?" Even whispering, Alice's words echoed in the room.

"It used to be the Wizard's waiting room. People from all over Oz would come and wait for an audience with him. He was very reclusive; so many people waited in vain." Brax didn't bother to whisper, allowing the echo to fill the vast room. "When the Council came to power, this room, and the Throne Room beyond it, weren't used. They preferred to set up their own governing chamber a few floors down, so as not to live in the shadows of Oz's former rulers. This place became a museum of sorts."

"Yes." Glinda broke away from her quiet conversation with Jellia. "That was the beginning of the Council choosing to turn away from Oz's past, thinking that in order to forge into the future we had to forget what came before it." It wasn't hard to miss Glinda's disdain.

"Not everyone has turned their back on the past though." Again Jellia turned on her heel and began walking across the room.

The others followed her to the set of doors that must

have been the entrance of the Throne Room Brax had mentioned. Instead of going through the doors, however, she stepped over to the side, to an empty section of the wall.

Jellia placed her hand flat on the wall and closed her eyes. Nothing happened, at least nothing that Alice could see. After waiting with baited breath, she began to feel a little silly standing there, watching expectantly. Even Scarecrow couldn't stand still. But then, just as Alice was going to ask if something was wrong, the solid stone of the wall began to melt beneath Jellia's fingers, turning into a thick liquid. Instead of splashing on the floor, the substance parted down the middle and merged with the walls, revealing a small opening.

Inside what had once been solid wall, sat a small ring. The band was gold with a brilliant, red ruby set into it. At first glance, it looked quite ordinary. Alice had to wonder why it required such a hiding place. But as she stepped forward to get a closer look, the ruby began to glow with a light that came from deep within the jewel. A peculiar tingling sensation in her feet made her gasp. Looking down, she found that her shoes had begun to shine as well. A heat filled her body that could only be described as magical. She could feel the power of the relics radiating inside.

"The Heart of Ozma," Jellia said, awed. "This chamber

hasn't been opened since the ring was put here shortly after the completion of the palace. Not even the Wizard knew its location. It is one of Oz's most guarded secrets."

"The legend says that when the Fairy Queen's daughter, Ozma, died, her body vanished into mist, leaving only this ruby filled with the entirety of her magic. No one knows its true origin, but people enjoy the romantic tale. Alice, will you please try to retrieve it." She had been waiting for Glinda to ask, just like she had done back in the rundown house with the crystal.

As her hand wrapped around the ruby ring, the tingling in her shoes became a jolt. The glowing light began to pulse, growing brighter and brighter. Combined with the light of the shoes, it created a brightness that drowned out everything around them. Instead of burning her eyes, however, it filled Alice with a sense of relief and contentment. She inhaled deeply, sighing as she released her breath.

The feeling faded the second Glinda took the ring from Alice's hand. The light around them returned to normal, leaving spots in their eyes. Alice shook her head to clear her mind of that feeling. She had to admit that it was pleasant, but at the same time, felt awkward and false. It left her a little uneasy. She was glad to see Glinda place the ring in the same bag that held the crystal.

"That's three of the relics brought together now. Their

power is strengthening. I can feel it. The fourth, and final, one will be the most difficult to obtain. It would have simplified matters if she had not stolen it from this very room, but..."

Stepping away, Alice let Glinda's voice fade away from her ears. She needed a moment to clear her head. The sensation of magic had rattled her a bit. In her whole life, not even in Wonderland, had she ever felt anything remotely similar. It was a curious feeling, both powerful and frightening. Was that what Glinda felt all the time with her magic?

Alice made her way to the center of the room, where the statue stood. It was clearly meant to be the centerpiece, towering over the other podiums. She looked up, taking the whole thing in. It was a remarkable likeness of a girl, standing with her feet spread apart, mid step. A basket hung from the crook of her left arm. The dress, so perfectly crafted, seemed to be frozen as if caught in a phantom breeze. The only thing not perfect was the face. It was disfigured and melted beyond all recognition underneath two golden braids. Alice did not need to read the plaque at the statue's feet to know who she was looking at.

Dorothy.

"It's absolutely hideous, isn't it?"

She froze, her heart immediately beating faster in her

chest. The silky, smooth voice made her blood run cold. It was not the sound of any of her companions. None of them could come close to sounding so beautiful and so dangerous at the same time. "The Ozians do love their hero worship, tacky as it may be."

Alice couldn't move out of fear. A tickle ran up the back of her neck as she sensed a presence so very close behind her. The soft, slow clack of shoes echoed against the emerald floor. In her petrified state, Alice watched the woman come into her line of sight and her breath threatened to choke her.

The only visible part of the Witch's face was a pair of ruby red lips twisted into a smirk. The rest of her features were obscured by the shadows of a dark green hood attached to a thick cloak draped over her shoulders. Underneath, a simple black dress hugged the curves of her body. She was majestically beautiful and immensely terrifying.

"You must be the Alice I have been hearing so much about." The Witch's smile stretched. "What a pleasure to finally meet you."

Alice found her voice, but only enough to release a small scream that echoed throughout the vast room.

The others, still by the opening in the wall, alerted by Alice's shout all turned in her direction. "No!" Glinda shouted. It was Brax who had snapped into action first. He ran as fast as his feet would take him at the Witch, who showed no concern.

As if bored, the Witch waved a hand and Brax was immediately knocked backwards, landing hard on the floor. Alice had thought he was merely thrown back, but when Glinda got closer, she was stopped by something invisible. Her hands pressed hard into a wall that was not really there. Alice gave another fearful cry.

"It's a simple barrier spell. No harm will come to them. That isn't why I have come." The Witch moved to the base of the statue. She sat next to one of Dorothy's feet and crossed her legs. Without being able to see into her eyes, Alice couldn't read the Witch's expression, but she could feel the dangerous power radiating from her.

"Why did you come here then?" There was no stopping the quiver in her voice. To hide the fact that they were shaking, she hid her hands behind her back.

"To meet you, of course. It's not every day that Glinda stupidly pulls someone from the Other Land in an attempt to stop me. I was curious."

"Curious enough to lay waste to the Eastern province of Oz to find me?"

The Witch shrugged her shoulders dismissively. "They should have told me where you were going. But it's no matter. I

[181]

knew where I would eventually find you. All visitors make their way to the Emerald City."

"And why was it so important to meet me?" Alice could think of nothing else to say. Her only plan was to stall, hoping to give Glinda time to break through the barrier and come to her aid. She was not prepared to take on the Witch alone.

"Please, Alice, get that scared look off your face. I am not here to hurt you. I came here simply to talk. And perhaps to warn you."

Alice was ready to jump from her skin. She wanted to run, but knew there was no point. The wall that kept the others out would surely keep her in. And she desperately did not want to anger the Witch.

"Leave her alone!" Glinda's cry came through the barrier muffled, but clear enough to be heard. Her fists pounded ineffectually against the wall. The frantic look on her face did not ease Alice's racing mind.

The Witch stood abruptly, her smile melting into a scowl of distaste. "Oh, Glinda, do shut up." She waved her arm violently through the air and the effect was immediate. Glinda clutched her throat, her mouth still moving but producing no sound. Turning back to Alice, she said, "She always did talk too much, don't you think?"

"Warn me against what?" Alice shouted the question,

mostly to get the Witch's attention off her companions, afraid of what she would do to them.

Her scowl faded, replaced with another smile. "Your choice of friends. Oz is a dangerous place and you have to be careful within whom you put your trust. Not everyone has your best interests in mind."

"But you do?"

Her laugh was not the cackle Alice had imagined, but the Witch was not living up to her story book expectations. "Perhaps not. It's no secret that I want you gone from Oz. But that does not necessarily mean I have to kill you." She stepped closer, much closer than Alice was comfortable with. The finger that ran along her chin made her skin crawl. "Don't mistake me though, if I have to I will, but that could be extremely...messy."

"Why not send me home then?" It was a bold move. She had thought about going back to Oxford, but knew that Glinda would not have allowed it. But the Witch was standing in front of her. They could both get what they wanted. Would she be content enough with just sending Alice away?

"If that were within my power, don't you think you would be there already instead of standing here, talking to me?" The Witch circled around her, a predator stalking its prey. "But there is another way, a much easier way. One that I am certain your good friend Glinda did not tell you about."

A cold sweat broke out on Alice's forehead. She did not like what she was hearing. It wouldn't surprise her to discover that Glinda was holding more back, but a way home? "What are you talking about?"

"The shoes." The Witch pointed to Alice's feet. "They've had the power to take you home since the moment you slipped them on your pretty little feet. Glinda likes to keep that to herself. But I am surprised that no one else has informed you. It's well known magic."

Alice looked down at the shoes glittering on her feet. She had been wearing them for days and they could have taken her home at any time. She could have been spared all of the horrible things she had experienced. Looking over at Glinda, who still struggled to make her voice work, Alice narrowed her eyes. Then she looked over at Brax. He stood there, not trying to fight against the wall, staring at her. When their eyes met, his eyes were sad, as if he knew exactly what the Witch was telling her.

Turning back to the Witch. "What do I have to do? How does the magic of the shoes work?"

The Witch's smile grew, apparently pleased. "It's rather simple. Tap your heels together three times and envision the place that you most wish to be. You can mutter some nonsense about home, but that's quite unnecessary. The shoes will do the rest."

Alice looked down at the shoes again. Was it really that easy? A magic wish and she would be safe in her bed, far away from Oz? How much time had passed in Oxford since she left? Were her parents frantic with worry? All of her answers were just three heel taps away. She raised herself up to her toes. Her heels moved together, but she paused when the Witch took a sharp intake of breath.

Lowering herself, she looked hard into the Witch's face, unsuccessfully trying to see through the impossibly dark shadows of her hood. "What happens to Oz and all of its people when I'm gone?"

The Witch tilted her head, uncomprehendingly. "The same thing that will happen should you stay. The only difference is that you will not be one of the fallen. It should not be that hard of a choice, Alice."

Her heart beat so hard in her chest, she thought it might snap a bone. Somehow, she mustered up the courage to step closer to the statue, away from the Witch. "I don't understand. You have destroyed almost every part of Oz? Why? What's the purpose of ruining a place that you want to control? You will be ruling over ashes."

"You misunderstand me. I have no desire to rule this land. My only wish is to destroy Oz and everything in it." The sheer malice in her voice gave Alice an even deeper chill. There was such hatred there, a coldness that Alice could never fathom.

"But...but why? What have they done to deserve this punishment?"

Before the Witch could answer, the floor beneath shook violently, almost knocking Alice from her feet. A crack had formed along the green surface. The Witch studied the fractured floor before looking up at the others. Alice followed her gaze to find Glinda and Jellia attacking the invisible barrier. A red stream of fire shot forth from Jellia's hands combining with an icy blue light coming from Glinda's before slamming into the Witch's spell. The air shimmered in the heat.

"A story for another time. It appears your friends are only moments from breaking through and I have no intention of being here when they do."

With a graceful flick of her hand, a dark greenish smoke filled the air around it. It moved angrily, like boiling water. The Witch blew a breath towards it and the smoke faded away. In its place, a simple broom had appeared clutched tightly in her fingers. It was old, obviously hand made. The bristles were blackened and burnt at the tips.

Dropping it to the ground with a clatter, she stepped on, balancing perfectly on the thin handle. "Think hard about what I told you. I'll give you some time to decide, but don't take too long. Use the shoes. And do not trust Glinda."

The broom rose into the air, climbing higher and higher. Alice simply watched as the Witch neared the ceiling and disappeared through one of the circular windows close to the top. Long after she had gone, Alice continued to stare. The pounding of her heart in her ears drowned out all other thoughts.

It was the touch of Brax's hand on her shoulder that brought her back to herself. She turned and met his eyes, but could say nothing. Thought would not form. Everything that the Witch had told her fought for space in her mind. It only got worse when Glinda appeared by her side and a wave of revulsion passed over her.

"It's okay, Alice. She's gone." Brax's hand moved to her hair and gently rubbed the back of her head. While comforting, it did not ease her thoughts.

She looked from Brax to Glinda and back again. "I want to leave." Her problem was she could not be sure if she meant the palace, the city, or Oz itself.

Chapter 15

The Emerald City grew smaller behind them. As it slowly slipped further and further to the horizon, the tightness in Alice's chest loosened. She would only be happy when she could no longer see the tops of the buildings in the sky. Then she hoped to forget her time there. Though she did not think where they were headed was going to be any more pleasant.

Jellia had opted not to join the group on their journey. "There's no point in my staying here in the palace any longer, with nothing to guard. I'd like to see Gillikin Country again, even in its current state." So Scarecrow volunteered to escort Jellia back to the Council's safe house with the promise of meeting up with them later. Alice had no idea how he could accomplish such a thing until Glinda waved her hand and produced a small glass sphere with white mist roiling around inside.

"Smash this and the smoke will transport you back to us. Be mindful with it. I do not have enough magic to make another or to get you across Oz by other means." It was a relief when it was Jellia, not Scarecrow, who took hold of the ball and held it to her chest.

Before they departed, Jellia had lead them down to the

lowest level of the palace where they found the most bizarre stable. Carriages occupied the stalls instead of horses. Alice walked up to the closest one and it rolled away, slamming into the back of its stall. She jumped, already on edge, not expecting the carriage to have a life of its own.

"Not that one, dear, she's quite temperamental. That was the Wizard's personal transport. No has been able to ride in her since the Wizard became a hermit." Glinda was running her hand along the side of a white carriage with gold trim. It seemed to be pushing itself closer to the woman. "This is the one we will be taking. Since I won't have enough magic to take us there, we will have to settle for traveling on ground."

Alice let out a silent sigh of relief. She was not fond of the idea of being in that enclosed bubble with Glinda. She had not said a word to the woman since the Witch's departure, and she did not intend to. Too many conflicting emotions battled within Alice. At least in an open carriage it would be easier to shift her focus. And, she could not lie, it eased her mind knowing that, at least for a while, Glinda would be without her magic.

After what felt like an eternity, they made their exit from the Emerald City. It was slow going at first because the carriage had a difficult time navigating the crumbling road.

Many of the yellow bricks were missing, leaving large spaces to maneuver around. It led to a rather bumpy ride, but Alice was too busy watching the city disappear to notice that or Glinda's incessant chatter.

"The West has always been one of the most dangerous places in all of Oz. Because the Wicked Witch of the West ruled over it so severely, many people feared to cross its borders. Since the Fall of the Wicked, there have been attempts to tame the land, like the Yellow Brick Expansion. But with the Witch making the West her home territory, it has been effectively cut off from the rest of Oz again."

Alice wasn't sure who Glinda was talking to. Brax had his eyes closed and leaned against the back of the seat. He knew everything as it was. And she had to know that Alice was in no mood. Perhaps she was just talking because the silence made her uncomfortable. Whatever the reason, Alice halfway wished that the Witch's spell hadn't worn off and Glinda was still cursed into silence.

Once they had crossed the border into the West, the road was far less damaged, allowing for a smoother trip. Alice took the opportunity to place her head against the plush cushion. If she was lucky, she would be able to rest until they reached wherever it was they were going.

And she would have, if not for the storm.

It came out of nowhere. Dark, angry clouds rolled in, covering the murky gray ones that hung overhead. The thunder clapped so hard that the ground beneath the carriage wheels shook slightly. Lightening left white spots in Alice's vision when she blinked. The fierceness with which it appeared marked it as unnatural and magic made. Witch made.

Glinda insisted that they keep moving, that the weather should not hinder their progress, but Brax disagreed. Alice had no opinion because she was positive that neither of them would have listened to it. Brax's demand for shelter won out, even though Glinda was not pleased to be stopping. They managed to take cover under a twisted knot of trees just as heavy raindrops began to fall.

Glinda had left them there, off to perform whatever ritual it was to restore her magic to its full strength. "If the Witch is sending enchanted storms to block our path, it would be best to have something useful to fight her with."

Alice didn't care what the reason, she was just thankful that Glinda was gone, no matter how short a time it would be. She felt infinitely more comfortable in her absence.

"You did well against the Witch. You should be proud of yourself."

Alice looked at Brax in disbelief. Because of the

darkness brought on by the storm, it was difficult to make out his face, but she managed well enough. "What are you talking about? I did nothing. She talked and I stood, frozen."

"That is much more than some people could do. I have seen people lose themselves and beg for mercy at the mere threat of the Witch. You stood your ground. It was impressive."

"It didn't feel that way at the time. Just being near her was terrifying." Alice shifted on the dirt, attempted to find a comfortable position on the hard ground. She let the silence stretch out for a moment before speaking again. "You know what she told me. Is it true?" She knew the answer, of course, but she needed to hear it from him to be absolutely sure.

Brax was quiet for a moment. His eyes focused on the sheet of rain through the opening in their shelter. "The shoes can take you home. It's part of their magic. They can grant you the wish of going anywhere you desire. It's the same way Dorothy left Oz after her travels."

She sat for a moment, absorbing his words. It was what she had expected so she didn't know why a weight dropped in her stomach. "Why didn't Glinda tell me? Why hasn't anyone told me? Why haven't you?"

"Because of the thoughts that have been running through your head since the Witch told you the truth. We were afraid that you would click your heels together and vanish from

[192]

Oz, taking away our only chance to end this nightmare. It cost a lot to bring you here, even if it was not what we intended. We could not take that risk."

"Has it occurred to anyone to have a little faith in me? You are asking this great service of me, yet have no trust."

"I can only speak for myself, but I have learned my lesson. I have underestimated you. When you first arrived, I truly did not believe you up to this task. I was wrong. And for that, I apologize. I promise to be more forthcoming from now on. You have earned that much from me."

Alice's fingers clawed at the dirt beneath her legs. "I wish the same could be said about Glinda."

Brax released a heavy sigh. "Glinda." Brax turned slightly until he was facing Alice. "Do not judge her too harshly. I know it's easy to do. But her intentions are good."

She scoffed and turned away. "My mother liked to say 'The road to Hell is paved with good intentions.'"

"Your mother may be right, but she doesn't live in Oz, does she?" His words were coarse, but not cold. "Glinda does."

"But what is wrong with that woman? Why are all of her actions blanketed with secrets and lies?" Alice did not bother to hide the exasperation in her voice. She had seen and been told too much to feel any other way.

[193]

"Can't you see how difficult this has been for her? She is Glinda the Good Witch."

Alice interrupted him before he could say anything further. "Exactly. She's supposed to be good. But she doesn't act like it. From what I have seen, she behaves profoundly wicked."

"The line between good and wicked is not as clear as it once was. You used to be able to look around and see the difference plain as the day. But nothing is the same. It's not only the land that has been twisted and corrupted by the Witch. Glinda is doing what she feels she must."

"That is a small comfort to the person being deceived." Alice stood, unable to contain the nervous energy in her legs. Unfortunately, the shelter's ceiling was too low for her to stand straight, forcing her to hunch over. It brought back unpleasant memories of not only Wonderland, but of the underground tunnel.

"Alice, I am not asking you to forgive Glinda." Brax tried to stand, but being taller than Alice, he could barely rise from his knees. He crouched in front of her, hands reaching out to hers. "I'm not even asking you to trust her. I'm merely asking that you understand her. She feels personally responsible for what has befallen Oz. She is doing everything in her power to try to repair the damage, even if her methods come across as a little questionable."

Conflict flashed across Alice's face. She hoped that Brax couldn't see it in the dark. She wanted to understand Glinda's reasons, but compassion was hard to grasp when faced with all the lies and danger. Would it have been that hard for Glinda to just offer the smallest warning before sending Alice out into the hostile environment?

Brax's pleading tone made her resolve to stay angry falter. Since she had met him, he had been the cold, strong warrior of the group. For him to beg on Glinda's behalf made it important. If he could do such a thing, then maybe she could try to let go of some of her anger. She could try to understand, even if she was more confused than ever.

But at the same time, she expected a little more honesty. Glinda knew that Alice was finally aware of the power in the shoes. She had to see that if Alice was going to use them, she would have done so already. The idea still lingered in the back of her mind, but she knew that she wouldn't. It would not be the honorable thing to do. She had made Glinda, and all the people of Oz, a promise. Despite how terrifying the prospect was becoming, she would not turn her back on that.

She gave Brax a small, almost imperceptible, nod of her head. "I'll try. But I expect you, at the very least, to be more forthcoming and honest with me."

"You have my word." He gave her hands a light pull, bringing her back to the ground with him. "You should sit. You have had a very trying day and need your rest."

As she sat, he pulled her closer to him until her head rested on his shoulder. An arm moved around her, tightening its hold. It only took moments for a sense of comfort to wash over her. In another moment she was asleep. For the first time, she felt something she did not think was possible in Oz. Safe.

Chapter 16

Yellow bricks gave way to patches of dirt that had been carved into makeshift paths. Construction on the road must not have been able to go any further at that point. Alice looked around the landscape, taking in the differences. Much of what she had seen so far had been ruins, but the land at least looked to have been inhabited. Houses, structures, farms, people. But the West was completely different.

There was no destruction, just a lush wilderness that stretched as far as Alice could see. Trees towered over the land, reaching for the sky. But there was no sign that anyone lived there. It was the closest thing Alice had ever seen to an untouched piece of land. She was sure that there were people and animals, but they did a good job of leaving no trace.

"Don't let the peace mislead you. The West is quite possibly the most dangerous part of Oz." Brax stood next to Alice and stared at the expanse of forest before them. In an attempt to keep his word, he had been giving her as much information about the area as they grew closer.

She didn't see how the tranquil land in front of her

could be so full of danger, but she did know that looks could be deceiving. It was, after all, the place that the Witch had chosen to inhabit. "Other than the Witch's presence, what makes this place so dangerous?"

"The Winkies." Glinda stepped to the other side of Alice. She did not find herself instinctively moving away from the woman as she had earlier. Part of her still wanted to, but she kept still. She promised Brax she would try. "The Winkies dominate this section of Oz. They are a fierce people who have lived most of their lives in one form of slavery or another. They have only known the small time of freedom that lasted from the Fall of the Wicked to the Witch's rise. Their anger regarding their constant enslavement only makes them more of a threat. Since they cannot take down their master, they have become indifferent as to who they cause harm, as long as someone suffers at their hands."

"That's barbaric." She couldn't imagine people harming others simply because they were unhappy with their lot in life. The forced enslavement they lived under must have been horrible. Alice surely felt sorry for them, but did that give them an appropriate excuse to hurt others, especially those who were not to blame?

"That is life in Western Oz. And unfortunately, that is not all the Witch's doing. It has been this way here for a very

[198]

long time." There was definitely a hint of regret in Glinda's voice. Alice felt a small twinge of sympathy pulling at her heart. Even though she was still distrustful, she was gaining compassion towards the woman. "Hopefully, we can change that." A small, but sincere, smile crossed Glinda's lips.

That smile gave Alice a little harder push towards understanding. Glinda looked on Oz as a mother would over a child. And the land was hurting. One didn't have to look hard to see the hurt that lingered in Glinda's eyes. Could Alice honestly say that she would not feel the same way, and possibly act the same, if she were in Glinda's position?

"So, we are off to the Witch's castle?"

"Yes, that is where we will find the last of the relics. It is in the Witch's possession. Once it was housed in the Wizard's Palace, but after attacking the Emerald City, the Witch stole it."

"What is it? If she took this one, why didn't she try for the others?"

Out of the corner of her eye, Alice could see Brax give a small approving nod. Accompanied with the trace of a smile, she took it to mean he was pleased with her thinking. For some reason that she couldn't quite explain, that made her stomach twist into knots.

"The last relic is a tree that is said to be the first to ever grow in Oz. Since it was the first of its kind, it soaked up the magic directly from the land itself. For many years, The Ozian Tree of Life was worshipped by almost everyone. People would journey from all four corners to bask in its power and hope that it might grant their deepest wishes."

"A tree?" Alice asked, incredulous. She had a hard time picturing themselves carrying an entire tree for the rest of the journey. How else were they supposed to access the great magical power that came from uniting the relics if they weren't able to bring the tree with them? She had a hard time believing that, even by magical means, it would fit in the small sack in which Glinda carried the other relics.

"Do not worry. It is not a tree any longer. Some years ago, a group of wicked witches harnessed the power of the tree. They chopped it down, dividing it amongst themselves. Each used the wood to craft a magical broom that possessed all of the powers contained in the tree. Over time, the brooms vanished from history, along with the wicked witches who possessed them. The only remaining one known to exist belonged to the Wicked Witch of the West. After Dorothy defeated her, the broom sat on display as a trophy in the Wizard's Audience Room. But now it is in the Witch's hands." Glinda took a step on the path, testing the ground before taking another. Alice and Brax followed behind her. "I'm more certain than ever that she does not know the importance of the broom. From her actions, she is content only to cause as much damage as she can. I don't believe she cares much about the underlying magic of Oz. The broom is simply a symbol of power to her and nothing more."

The group fell silent as they followed a barely visible dirt path leading into the forest before them. Alice used the silence to ponder Glinda's words. "She is content only to cause as much damage as she can." The Witch had all but said the same thing to her in the Emerald City. Alice could not get her mind around the idea of causing so much harm with no real motive.

The trees were on them before Alice realized it. They began walking through the twisted trunks, the path even harder to discern. The forest was not like the Dead Woods. While the roots and trunks were wilder and more gnarled, the canopy of leaves allowed more of the sickly gray light through. A small part of Alice wished for the pitch blackness from before, as not to see her ominous surroundings in such stark detail.

And if the area was darker, then perhaps she could have continued walking for much longer before noticing the many pairs of eyes watching her through the leafy growth. The Winkies were skilled at concealing themselves. Alice assumed they had a great deal of practice during their many years of enslavement. At first, she could only make out eyes peering at them, but she soon began to see bodies hiding amid the trunks. Some were perched high up in the trees, looking down on them with odd expressions. It was apparent that they were surrounded in all directions.

Glinda appeared to be oblivious to what was going on around them. She walked with a purposeful stride, eyes fixed directly in front of her. Alice wanted to make her aware of the Winkie presence, but she was too nervous to make a noise. Perhaps if she just stayed quiet and feigned ignorance, they would be able to continue walking unmolested. She feared any sound would cause the Winkies to attack.

"The worst thing you can do right now is panic. They are holding their position and gathering information on us." Even speaking, Glinda held herself as if she didn't know they were in danger. "They aren't likely to attack us right away, not unless we give them a reason to."

That was easy for Glinda to say, but much harder for Alice to do. With each new pair of eyes that appeared, her heart beat faster and faster. She placed a hand on her chest but it did little to calm her down. The Winkies were there on orders from the Witch, but what were their instructions? To capture or to kill?

A gentle hand found its way to the small of her back.

Brax stood closely behind her, guiding her with his steps. "It's okay, Alice."

"But..."

"Shhh. They can hear the fear in your voice. They will see that as weakness."

Alice closed her eyes and let herself be led by Brax. She tried to remember happier times, anything to ease her nerves. If she could just control herself, then possibly the Winkies watching her would not be able to sense the dreadful fear building up inside her. But, that was also easier said than done.

She looked down at the jeweled shoes on her feet. Somehow they still managed to sparkle even in the absence of direct sunlight. How easy would it be to click her heels together? Did the Witch know how tempted Alice would be? To have the power to return home so close, but to know that she shouldn't use it. It was simply another way the Land of Oz had of torturing her.

Her calming techniques failed, but she was able to continue following Glinda. Alice had to admit, despite her attempts, she still did not like the woman much, but it was admirable how she walked on without the smallest hesitation. Alice may have questioned some of her actions, but there was no denying Glinda's bravery.

[203]

The trees began to thin out, leaving more room for them to walk. It wasn't long before the path led them into a small clearing. The roots of the trees rose up to build a circular wall, stretching all the way around. Small openings, like doors, were interspersed throughout. Even with her limited knowledge of such things, Alice was aware they were walking into a trap.

Sure enough, as soon as they had stepped fully into the clearing, Winkies started appearing out of the shadows. Their camouflage was so perfect it was as if they were forming out of thin air. Now that she could see them clearly, she could also make out the various types of weapons they held. Axes, swords, bows, and even large sticks. Seeing they had come armed did not help to calm Alice down.

"Keep walking. Just take it slow." Glinda did not wait to see if her words would be acknowledged or not, she continued walking like there was not an army of hostile Winkies blocking their way.

If it weren't for the constant presence of Brax's hand on her back, Alice was unsure if she would have kept walking to the center of the clearing. Each eye felt like it pierced her skin. If only she could channel some of Glinda's nerve.

Glinda raised her hand, signaling them to stop while she continued to walk. Alice watched as the gathered Winkies looked from one to the other. With a small nod of his head, the one standing directly in front of Glinda stepped forward as well. With small, measured steps, they met in the exact center of the clearing.

"We must pass." Alice and Brax stood close enough that they were able to hear Glinda's words clearly. "I know that you have been ordered to stop us, but we must get to the Witch's castle."

"We cannot allow that." The lead Winkie's voice was deep and hoarse, as if from disuse. "You know that we cannot disobey a direct order. The chains that bind us are tight."

"If you let us pass, then we might be able to release you from those chains." Glinda remained calm and spoke in soothing tones. Her hands hung in the air, palms up, to show that magic would not be used on them.

"We have heard all of this before, Glinda. Many before have tried to give us our freedom and failed. What makes that girl," he pointed an accusatory finger at Alice, "any different?"

Alice took offense at his tone. It struck her as odd that she could feel so insulted by a man leading a group of fighters determined to harm her. The Witch may have been controlling his actions, but not his words. Didn't he realize what Alice was trying to do? Did he have to sound so ungrateful?

Maybe it was his rude manner, or maybe it was some

inner bravery that Alice had managed to tap into, but something made her step forward. She stood level with Glinda and looked at the Winkie in front of her. Then she swept her eyes around the clearing, taking in all the Winkies fighters. They waited with expectant eyes.

"I'm sorry for what you have been through. It hurts me to think of you as slaves to such a malicious master. I cannot promise this will be the end of your enslavement, that I will be successful in stopping the Witch. But I can promise you that I will try." She took another step forward, taking the lead. "I was brought here against my will with no knowledge of the conditions of this land. I have been given the ability to go home, to save myself, and leave you all to whatever fate the Witch desires. But I choose not to take it. I have chosen to make your fight my own. Allow us to pass and I will do everything in my power to help you." Alice had merely started talking to free them of the situation, but as the words came out, she realized the truth in them. She would not leave the people of Oz to suffer. She knew that she wouldn't from that first hesitation in the Wizard's Palace. It had truly become her mission, and not just something forced on her by trickery.

The Winkies murmured amongst themselves. Weapons were raised and lowered again as they spoke to one another. The leader turned to face his fighters as their grumbles grew louder. He made a small, barely noticeable, nod before turning back to face Alice directly.

"You may pass." As soon as he said it, a dark green aura formed around him. The light pulsed angrily. Pain filled the leader's face as his knees gave out on him. He sank to the leaf strewn ground and clutched the dirt with shaking hands.

Looking around, Alice could see all the Winkies having the same reaction. Surrounded by the same pulsing, green light, their weapons fell as their bodies were wracked with pain. Only a few were able to remain on their feet, while most had fallen to the ground. Some weren't even able to stay conscious, passing out from whatever pain they were experiencing.

"Go." The lead Winkie croaked. "We may...not...fight...magic...long."

Glinda snapped into action. Grabbing hold of Alice's arm, she roughly dragged her away from the Winkie. Alice had trouble keeping up because she couldn't tear her eyes away from the Winkie's torment. Her feet caught on grounded twigs or twisted roots several times, but Brax was there to stabilize her and keep her moving. "What's happening to them?" She called out as they ran.

"They disobeyed an order from the Witch. The magic that binds them is trying to force them to follow her will.

[207]

Fighting it is costing them a great deal." Glinda explained, not looking back. Her grip on Alice's arm did not loosen, but tightened harder. "Run, Alice. They will not be able to fight the spell much longer."

Alice forced herself to take control of her feet. She matched Glinda's steps, weaving around the tree roots and trunks. Brax kept pace behind them. Alice could see that he had pulled his axe out and had it ready.

Behind them, an ear piercing scream of pain tore through the air, followed by several more. The Winkies were being tortured by magic. Part of Alice yearned to go back to help them, but Glinda's grip would not permit it.

"They will be coming soon. We must hurry." Even Alice could not miss the panic in Glinda's voice.

Chapter 17

They ran for a long time, so long that Alice had lost track. The forest passed in a blur. Glinda showed little concern about the low hanging branches in their path. Alice's arms and face were scratched repeatedly, but she was in such a panic that the pain barely registered. She would tend to it later, when there was time to worry about such things.

Occasionally, they could hear a clamoring behind them. The Winkies had finally succumbed to the magic that drove them to obey their orders. Each time their pursuers gained on them, Glinda waved her hand and a strong wind rushed past them. "The masking spell will only hold them back for a short time. We must keep going."

So they did. They ran through the trees with little care of which direction they were going. There was no path for them to follow. Their only concern was to escape. For a brief second, Alice wondered if they might be heading further away from their destination, not towards it. But those thoughts were quickly pushed aside at the sound of a Winkie crashing through the trees behind them. They would be even angrier, more fearsome, after the Witch's magic had punished them for their disobedience. Would they have any control over themselves anymore? The Witch may have taken the last shreds of their free will away.

They entered a particularly dense section of the woods. The trees were so close together that their twisted roots wrapped around their neighbors. It was not the ideal place for running. Even Glinda had difficulty moving through, her dress catching on exposed brambles. Despite all that it had survived on their journey, the trees proved to be too much for it and rips started to form in the blue material.

Finally, when they reached the densest part of the trees yet, Glinda stopped. She sagged against the closest trunk, fighting to catch her breath. One hand held tightly to the bark of the tree, while the other clutched at her chest, unsuccessfully attempting to steady her breathing. Alice put her hands on her knees, seconds from vomiting on the forest floor. She shot Brax a small look of annoyance for not looking at all winded from their flight. He stood guard over the two gasping women while they were vulnerable.

With a great deal of effort, Glinda struggled to her feet just as the sound of their pursuers reached their ears. Alice grabbed her side tightly, knowing she would not be able to continue at that pace. Luckily for her, Glinda was not preparing to run. She stood between two trees, one hand pressed into the bark of each. A look of deep concentration replaced her pained expression. Eyes shut tight, small beads of sweat began to form on her brow. Even if Alice could pull in enough breath to speak, she knew better. Whatever Glinda was doing, it required no interruption.

The air between the two trees began to ripple. The closest comparison that Alice could make was the way the area around a fire becomes hazy from the heat. The effect spread until the entire space between the trees moved like air becoming liquid. A light mist swirled in the haze. Forming an almost tangible wall in front of them, it seeped past the trees taking up a wide area of the woods.

"Do. Not. Move." Glinda's words strained under the effort to hold up the wall of mist.

Brax's arms snaked around Alice, pulling her close and hugging her tight to his chest. She didn't understand why until five Winkies appeared, sprinting right at them. Brax was trying to ensure that she did not run off at the sight of them. But his precaution was quite unnecessary. She had the suspicion that, should she try to run, her shoes would not have allowed it. They would have kept her rooted to the spot because she was supposed to stay still. But more than that, she knew, even if she could attempt an escape, she wouldn't. Glinda had decided to make a stand and Alice was ready to do the same. She had no weapon to fight with, but that didn't change the fact that she was ready for whatever was to come.

But it never did. Just as their attackers reached Glinda's wall, they inexplicably turned off to the right and continued on. "I saw them over there. They're trying to circle back to where they entered the forest," the lead Winkie shouted, pointing off into the distance. He didn't even seem to notice the three of them standing mere feet away.

Alice looked around confused, then turned to Glinda. Her hands were pressed so hard into the trees that small trails of blood ran down her arms. Beneath her long skirt, Alice could see how badly her legs were shaking. It was taking a lot of effort for Glinda to simply remain standing. She only lasted a few more seconds before her entire body sagged. Brax and Alice rushed forward to help her.

"That should keep them chasing shadows for a while. We should be safe now." Glinda was so very weak, unable to hold her head up.

Alice looked up and met Brax's eyes. "There's no way that she can keep going."

Brax looked conflicted. They had to keep moving, but how? Glinda could barely keep her head up, much less continue on to the Witch's castle. The only alternative that they had was to drag Glinda through the trees which would take energy and time. And neither one of them imagined Glinda would approve of such a thing, no matter how dire the need.

"Her spell should be enough to keep them away. We can hide her in the trees. I will keep guard while you watch over her."

They managed to move her to a tight cluster of tree roots. It was not the best concealment they could have asked for, but it would do. Alice gathered as many leaves as she could to use as a makeshift pillow. Once again, far from perfect, but it would serve its purpose.

Brax moved off a little ways to stand guard, his axe raised. Alice watched him scan the immediate area, ready for any danger that might arise. She thought he made the picture of the model soldier, ever prepared to defend them. That sense of safety from earlier filled her chest again.

While Brax stood sentry, she sat in the dirt, next to Glinda's head. In sleep, the woman looked peaceful. The ever present worry and anger that followed her were gone. It was enough for Alice to imagine the Glinda from before, back when Oz was a wonderful place. She had to admit that, asleep, Glinda was more likeable. Alice could almost see past the lies and omissions, all the way to Glinda's true self. Without conscious thought, her fingers moved into Glinda's blond hair and slowly stroked her head, the same way her mother did when Alice was hot with fever.

She sat that way for a long while. What little light that was able to shine through the canopy of trees had grown brighter, signaling the arrival of midday. Alice knew time was of the essence and they had to get moving, but she did not rush or try to wake Glinda. Once it had become apparent that the Winkies were no longer on their trail, her sense of urgency had diminished. Alice felt comfortable enough to sit and give Glinda the time she needed to recover.

When her legs had grown stiff and she could be still no longer, Alice rose from the ground. Slowly, she made her way to where Brax stood watch. His eyes had not once left the trees, even though it had been some time since there had been any signs of life coming near them. Alice feared that if he stood any straighter, his spine would snap from the tension.

The only sign he showed of his being aware of her presence was the subtle change in his breathing. And it might have just been her imagination, but she thought she saw his posture relax a small fraction. While he did not lower the axe, his fingers loosened their grip on the handle.

"You meant what you said to the Winkies. There was a

difference in the way you spoke." He still averted his eyes, but the smallest trace of a smile crossed his lips.

"I did." They were the only two people awake in the area, but she still kept her voice low. Not because she feared attracting unwanted attention, but because the moment felt more private, calling for a more reserved atmosphere.

"So you have made your decision to stay with us?"

"It was not much of a decision. I am not sure I could live with myself if I left Oz in the hands of the Witch, knowing I could have helped stop her. As tempting as it still is to leave, it is not the right thing to do. It is simply a question of right and wrong, of cowardice and bravery. I chose to be brave like Glinda has been."

He turned his whole body to look at her with a serious expression. "Glinda is fearless, without a doubt. She has had to be over the years with all that she has faced. But bravery is not walking into danger without pause. True bravery is feeling that fear and still facing danger, like you have done. You have proven yourself without question, not only by your actions, but by your choices."

Alice blushed at his words. She wouldn't say anything was without question because she had constant doubts. Through every step of her journey, she had been plagued by a

[215]

constant terror. All of her childhood stories made the heroes sound so fearless, dashing into action without a second's thought. That was not how Alice saw herself, not in the slightest.

"Believe in yourself, Alice. Like you have made me."

He stepped even closer to her, his axe dropping to his side. The space between them shrank to nothing as his free hand reached up and touched her face. His rough thumb ran along the line of her chin. She stood perfectly still as his warm breath tickled her cheek. Her heart thumped, for once not from a chase. For some time, she had been denying the attraction to him that she had sensed, but with the constant obstacles, she was forced not to think on it. But in the quiet of the woods, with no interruption, they were finally free to allow themselves to face what was forming between them.

Before another thought could pass, his lips were on hers, pressing insistently. His hand held her head to him. Even if she wanted to break free, she couldn't. But that was not her plan. She wrapped her arms around his neck, pushing into him. She matched the intensity of his kiss, feeling something she had never experienced before.

Once she allowed herself to let go completely, she could admit that she had an attraction from the very beginning, despite his rudeness towards her. Something about him drew her in. She had tried so very hard to ignore it. How could she feel anything about someone so ill-mannered? But as an understanding grew between them, she could finally say to herself that there was a spark.

The minutes slipped by them. The rest of Oz disappeared from their minds. All that mattered at that moment was each other and the embrace they shared. Their kiss had become the only thing in the whole world to either of them.

And it might have remained so for much longer, if it had not been for the smallest clearing of the throat coming from behind them. Glinda had finally awoken from her sleep. She sat up, her back pressed into a tree trunk.

They quickly broke away from each other. Alice immediately felt the loss. She longed to ignore the presence of another person and return to Brax's arms, but she knew that was impossible. As strongly as she wanted it, she understood where her focus ought to lie. More important matters had to take precedence.

"Thank you for letting me rest. I was very drained from the effort."

Glinda saved everyone from an awkward situation by ignoring what she had awoken to find. Even so, Alice could feel the heat begin to rise in her cheeks. The same flush brightened Brax's face as he looked sheepishly at the ground.

"We really must continue now." Glinda groaned, pushing herself up from the hard ground. Her full strength had not returned, but she appeared to be ignoring that as well.

With slow movements, she turned her back to them and moved down the path a short ways. From her lack of speed, she was either unable to move any faster or she was giving them a small moment of privacy. Whatever the reason, they took advantage of the opportunity. Giving Alice a shy smile, Brax reached out his hand. Without hesitation, she curled her fingers around his and they both followed Glinda through the trees.

Chapter 18

It was only a short time later when they caught the first sight of their destination. They came to a spot where the forest floor made a gentle slope into lower land, allowing for an unobstructed view for miles. Reaching higher than the tallest of the trees, Alice could make out the turrets of a castle. Even from a distance, the rough, dark stone was clear. She was reminded of the medieval castles she saw in a book once when she and her sister, Lorina, went snooping in their father's library. It was not a place that Alice ever imagined daring to go near.

"Our way to the castle should be easy now. The Winkies are dispatched throughout the forest, chasing false trails, and the winged monkeys are occupied in other parts of Oz."

"But it will still be protected by the Witch herself?"

Glinda nodded. "Most assuredly. She would never leave her stronghold unprotected."

Alice examined the castle. Knowing the Witch would be inside did not make her any more inclined to go, but she also knew there was no other option. The relic, the last one, was inside and they needed it desperately. It came down to a matter of getting it out of the Witch's hands, not a simple task. But that mattered little. They had to find a way.

They pushed on through the woods. Alice kept her eyes to the horizon, wanting to keep sight of the highest towers of the castle as they grew ever closer. With each step, the walls loomed over them, ominous and foreboding. She understood why the Witch had taken it as her place of power. The building itself seemed threatening and uninviting, helpful qualities when one's main goal was to keep people away.

They began to notice a difference in the trees as they traveled deeper. The color of the trunks changed from an earthy brown to the darkest black. It was a wonder that they still had life in them. Their upper branches sagged to the ground, weighted down by some unseen force. "Oz's magic is the most tainted here. It's seeping into all of living things, corrupting them," Glinda explained. Her expression had turned sad when she looked at the blackened trees.

As if time had decided to speed up just for the simple fact that Alice wished it to slow down, the massive drawbridge of the castle stood before them. It lay open, covering the wide moat that separated them from their destination. To Alice, it looked like an open invitation to cross beneath its portcullis. And it most definitely looked too simple.

"Do you think the Witch knows we are here?"

"I should think so." Glinda eyed the wide open entrance to the castle. "By now, she will be able to tell the Winkies have not succeeded in capturing us. Her magic has most likely punished them severely for that failure. And now, she has left the door open for us to just walk in. We are where she wants us to be."

Brax's hand found its way into hers again and gave it a firm, yet reassuring, squeeze. She returned the gesture, but stopped herself from looking at him. It was not the time for such things. She promised that, somehow, there would be time. It only gave her more incentive to move onward. The only way to get to that time was to confront the Witch face to face.

That thought gave Alice the courage to be the first one to step towards the castle. Glinda always led the way, but she seemed a little hesitant to make a move. Alice couldn't say that she blamed her, not being keen to do it herself, but she simply had to remember Brax's words. Those, combined with the speech she had given the Winkies, she knew that it was her time to take the lead.

The wood creaked under her feet as she walked across the drawbridge. She forced herself not to look to either side at the deep ravine she stood over. Brax and Glinda were careful to follow her down the center of the wooden bridge, away from its unprotected edges. Her new found courage did not extend to bottomless drops. Her instincts told her it would not be the same as falling down that rabbit hole.

The arched door to the castle stood open like the mouth of a dark creature preparing to swallow them whole. The portcullis's sharp teeth looked ready to bite into them. Dark windows, like eyes, watched their progression inside. It wasn't until they had passed through the massive doorway that Alice could stop thinking of it as a giant monster.

The interior of the castle was no more inviting than the exterior. Jagged, brown stones formed high walls. The barren entrance hall was devoid of any human comforts, not even a stray chair. Except for a single torch in a corner, the only thing that wasn't a part of the castle itself was a smattering of silver shards discarded against the far wall.

Glinda slowly walked to where they lay and picked up one of the pieces, turning it over in her hand. With a horrified gasp, she immediately dropped the shard. When it hit the ground, a clanking sound like a tin cup echoed against the walls. A river of tears ran down Glinda's sickly face.

"What is it?" Alice did nothing to mask the echo her words created. What was the point in hiding their presence when the Witch already knew they were there?

"Nick." Glinda spoke in a choked whisper, the answer getting lost somewhere in her throat.

"The Tin Woodman, one of Dorothy's original companions," Brax explained in response to Alice's confusion. "Before leaving, the Wizard appointed him ruler of the West. He's been missing ever since the Witch arrived."

Alice cried out in horror as the realization sank in. Those small scraps of metal laying haphazardly on the floor had once been a person, the owner of the small house they visited in the Dead Woods. But there was no life left in the tin. "Was he the Witch's first victim?"

"Indeed he was."

They all turned quickly at the sound of the cold voice. The Witch stood at the top of a steep, stone staircase carved into the far wall.

"He left me no choice but to dispose of him, playing the hero to the very end the way he did. Sadly, the heart he was given did little to help him in the end. He shouldn't have put so much faith in a gift from that old fool, the Wizard." The air filled with her small laughter. Alice never imagined a sound so small could carry such malice in it.

"What did he do to you to deserve this?" Alice's scream shot across the room like a dagger.

[223]

The Witch slowly took a couple of steps down the staircase. She looked the same as she had in the Wizard's Palace, the form fitting black dress still covered by the dark green cloak. Her eyes stayed concealed beneath her hood. And grasped in her right hand, the broom they sought. "Oh, Alice, how I wish you had heeded my warning. It would have simplified everything if you only had the capacity to listen."

"This must stop." Glinda stepped forward, anger pouring out of her in waves. Reaching the base of the staircase, she made to climb them, but stopped mid step.

The Witch barely registered Glinda had spoken. "This no longer concerns you." With the smallest flick of her hand, she sent Glinda flying across the room. She slammed into the wall, winded, but still conscious.

Brax rushed to her aid, leaving Alice alone to face the Witch. "What is the point of this? What do you hope to accomplish?"

The Witch continued down the stairs in slow even steps. She moved with a threatening elegance. Even with the hood, Alice could feel the Witch's stare. "You know my goal. I told you as much at our last meeting."

"Yes, but not your motive."

Ruby red lips curled into a cruel smile. "My reasons are my own. The people of Oz have brought my wrath down upon

[224]

themselves. You had your chance to escape, but chose not to take it. Now it's too late, and you will die." The Witch paused. "But if you give me those shoes, I promise it will be painless."

"The shoes? What could you possibly want with these shoes?" A weight dropped in Alice's stomach. She had a pretty good idea as to the reason, but she would not let on. There was still a chance that the Witch did not know about the power of the four relics and, if that was the case, she didn't want to be the one to make her aware.

"Let's just say I want them for sentimental reasons. So, please, give them to me. We don't want to prolong this, now do we?" The Witch had reached the base of the stairs. She held out an unnaturally pale hand towards Alice, expectantly.

"I am not giving you the shoes. If you want them so badly, there is only one way for you to get them." Alice mimicked the stance she had seen Brax strike so many times. Spine stiff. Ready. Strong. She knew she would be unable to defend herself against whatever magic was used to attack her. But she also knew that she would hold steady, no matter what.

"That can be arranged, my dear."

The Witch took a threatening step closer, but Alice did not move an inch, and it had nothing to do with the shoes forcing her. A hand raised towards Alice, ready to call upon the unknown horrors at the Witch's command. Alice closed her eyes, not wanting to watch the violence that would befall her. 'Help. Please.' Her words rang through her own head.

She expected to feel pain as the magic ripped through her and tore the shoes from her feet, but it never came. Instead, she again felt the warm sensation coming from the shoes. The feeling did not stay contained at her feet, however. Faster than she was able to prepare, it filled her entire body and continued to build. The shoes' enchantment had been called forward, perhaps by her plea for help. Having never felt anything of that intensity before, Alice wasn't sure how long she would be able to contain it.

Just as she lost the battle and the magical energy flooded out of her, the Witch released her own power in the form of a deep green bolt of lightning. With everything she had, Alice tried to direct the awesome power towards the Witch. As she opened her eyes, she saw a pale blue light streaming out from her. In the exact center of the two, the magical energies collided with each other.

For a moment, it was not certain which would overpower the other. In midair, the two lights fought for dominance, growing in brightness. Both Alice and the Witch stood watching as the battle of magics raged between them. The castle, itself, started to quake at the magnitude of the fight.

The heat was immense. Alice wanted to back away, to escape from the terrible thing they had unleashed. Just as the glare had grown so great that even the Witch put a hand up to block her hooded face, it was over. The forces collapsed on themselves and disappeared from sight.

They only had a moment to stare in wonderment, however, before an explosive force erupted from the very spot the magical battle had taken place. It expanded outward with such power that it knocked Alice and the Witch from their feet and threw them to opposite sides of the room. Alice tried to maintain her composure even as the very breath was pushed from her lungs. She tried to call upon the magic again to save her from the fall that was only moments away, but her attempts failed. The shoes remained cold.

The landing was not gentle. Pain radiated from every part of her. She could feel each of the small cuts being made in her back as she slid across the jagged stone floor. An eternity of pain went by before she came to a stop near where Glinda was barely managing to get to her feet with Brax's assistance. A small cry escaped her as she rolled off her back and onto her side. With great effort, she willed her body to stand.

Her legs felt as weak as the straw that Scarecrow was stuffed with. It could only be by the grace of the shoes that she was able to keep on her feet.

Glinda reached out her arms and took Alice in them. "I...Alice...I..."

A grunt made all three of them stiffen. They looked over to see the Witch struggling to rise from the floor. She made several attempts, but her heeled boots slipped on the stone and she fell back weakly. Somehow, even with the blast, the Witch still managed to keep her face hidden underneath the hood. Alice had hoped to at least see her face after such an ordeal. Was the Witch hiding some hideous deformity?

Glinda's breath caught. On the ground, a short distance from where Alice had stood, lay the broom.

"Get it!"

Brax had already started moving when Glinda shouted her order. Alice was on her way as well, but a strong grip stopped her. "Not you. Stay close to me." In rushed movements, Glinda pulled each of the other relics out of the bag at her side. The ring fit easily onto Alice's finger, as if it had been designed specifically for her. On the front of her pinafore, Glinda placed the crystal, securing it by some magical means in the absence of a clasp. "There. You are almost ready."

Meanwhile, Brax had made it halfway across the room. The Witch, who had yet to regain her feet, saw what he was after. Slowly, she crawled in the direction of the broom, but she

[228]

was too far away to make it there before him. She reached out, calling on her power to pull it to her. Just as it made the first jerking motion towards her, Brax grabbed the handle, forcing it free from the magical grip.

"Alice, catch!" With a yell, he launched the broom high into the air.

Everything seemed to move in slow motion. Alice's own heartbeat pounded in her ears as the broom made its crawling progression across the room. She was only mildly aware of the Witch getting to her feet and beginning to run. But it was too late. The broom was too far away for her to stop it. Alice reached up, stretching her arm until it would go no further. The rough wood of the handle slammed into her hand and she curled her fingers around it, tightening her grasp until her knuckles grew pale.

And then, in a flash, the whole world went white.

Chapter 19

Alice stood on something hard. At least, she assumed she was standing since she wasn't falling, though she could not make out the floor. Or anything for the matter. She was surrounded by the purest white, stretching in all directions, as far as she could see. The whole world had becoming nothing, and everything. She tried to take a step, but with no frame of reference, she had no idea if she had actually moved.

"Welcome." A soft, feminine voice came from the air itself. Alice looked around her, but could not see anything other than the empty brightness. "It's a pleasure to finally meet you, Alice."

"Who are you? Where are you?"

The disembodied voice giggled, girlishly, a slightly musical sound. "I am Ozma, the magic of Oz."

Ozma? Hadn't she heard that name before? Didn't Glinda mention it? A myth concerning a fairy queen and her daughter? Was it the same person? Or another trick of the magic?

"There are many rumors concerning my existence. My story has been much changed over the years. No one has used the relics to communicate with me in a very long time. People have forgotten." The air in front of Alice began to shimmer. An object began to appear, a misty haze at first. It gradually grew more solid, until finally the figure of a young girl stood there. She was unnaturally beautiful. Brown curls cascaded down her head, framing a perfectly heart shaped face. Large eyes, the color of chocolate, shone brightly. "But, I still remain."

Alice stared in awe at the girl. "I don't understand."

Ozma clasped her hands in front of her, the epitome of innocence. "The magical energy of Oz is ancient, as old as the first imaginative powers that gave life to all lands, including your Wonderland. I am the guardian of that energy. I can be called forward to help in times of the greatest need. Times like now."

"But the Witch has corrupted the magic of Oz, why have you not come forward before?"

The girl smiled sadly. "The rules are very clear. I cannot act on my own, only through another. A person must assemble the four ancient relics to call upon my assistance. It takes a person of a certain character to collect all four. One must prove themselves worthy of my aid."

Alice questioned if she possessed those qualities, since it was Glinda who guided her through the collection process. But she also knew better than to argue the point, since she needed the help that only Ozma could give. Without her, Alice had very little chance of overcoming the Witch's power. "Can you help me win?"

"I cannot guarantee success, but I can certainly give you a fighting chance. The Witch is extremely powerful simply because she has twisted the magic to serve her own purposes. But I am able to access that same magic in its purest, rawest form. With luck, that should be enough to overpower her."

"But I don't know how to control the magic. I was barely able to do it the one and only time I have ever tried. How do you know I will fare better a second time?"

"Do not worry about that. You are merely a conduit. I will handle the control."

That sounded all well and good to Alice, but she had to wonder if it was necessary. Was an all-out magical battle the answer to Oz's problem? There had been some form of fighting in all corners of the land since the Witch had taken over and no one was any better for it. "Is battle the only way to defeat her?"

Ozma began to walk, circling around Alice. It wasn't a predatory gesture, as with the Witch, but an appraisal. "The Witch's weakness is the same one that many people share. The past. Sometimes it is as simple as removing the masks that we wear to expose who we really are in our core. Revealing her identity, deep down, may bring her buried past to the surface and, like so many people, she may not be able to face it."

"But how do I accomplish that?" How could she remind the Witch of her past when she knew nothing of it? No one seemed to know much of where the Witch came from, much less what her life had been like before. Of all the impossible tasks she had been given, that seemed to be out of the realm of possibility.

"I'm sure we will think of something. You are quite resourceful." Alice wished she could mimic Ozma's confident tone, but she couldn't. She had seen only a small portion of what the Witch was capable of and, with no discernable plan, she was unsure of the odds of success.

"Before we depart, I must caution you. What Glinda told you was true. The magic of Oz has always been vulnerable to those from the Other Land. But the reverse is true as well. Not being of Oz, visitors have no tolerance to the energy. Magic has a life of its own, and right now, it is angry. It screams for retribution against the vile perversion that it has suffered. You must resist its pull, no matter the temptation."

'How ominous,' thought Alice. She was not very concerned, however. Anger and rage to that extent had never been emotions she felt that much. They didn't serve much purpose other than to cloud one's judgment. Alice believed she had enough sense about her to avoid being drawn in.

"Now come, it is time for us to depose the Wicked Witch of Oz." Ozma held out both of her hands and Alice placed hers in them.

With another flash, the bright white intensified, making it impossible to even see Ozma any longer.

Chapter 20

Time had stood still while she had her conversation with Ozma. When she opened her eyes to find she was back in the stone entrance hall of the castle, everything was exactly the same as it had been. Brax and Glinda stood behind her, looking breathless with anticipation. The Witch was still running towards Alice in an uneven path.

The only difference was the storm boiling under Alice's skin. She could feel the powerful magic coursing through her every nerve. It wasn't like before, with the constant pressure, ready to explode at any moment. It was controlled, an inflamed mass of energy awaiting her command. She could hear the soft whisper of Ozma in the back of her head, calming the immense power.

She turned to the Witch, who still came at her from across the room. With one hand holding the broom, Alice held the other out. "Stop." Her voice sounded different. Amplified. Commanding. Magical.

The Witch obeyed, involuntarily, struggling to move her feet. "So, you've found yourself some real magic, have you?"

There was no smile or sneer, only hatred. With a snap of her fingers, the stone beneath her feet began to crumble into a fine dust, freeing her. Instead of continuing her forward charge at Alice, the Witch stood tall. "That may be, but it changes nothing. You are not equipped to take me on."

And with that, the attack began. Alice barely had time to produce a barrier between them to block the first massive bolt of energy unleashed. Even then, the force of it pushed her back a couple of feet, but the shield held strong. The Witch would not be denied, however. It seemed like she was discharging the worst of her power in short, violent bursts. Balls of green fire. Streaks of green lightening. Pure green energy. One after the other, they slammed into the protective shield. Alice could feel it weakening from the assault.

When she knew it would not hold another second, she let it fade from existence. At the same time, the Witch launched a massive ball of fire with an inhuman scream. Green flames streaked dangerously towards Alice, but she made no move to avoid them. Instead, she trusted in the magic and the control that Ozma had promised. With a small twist of her wrist, she halted the fire in midair and reversed its direction. Having no time to react, the flames struck the Witch hard, knocking her back several feet. It was Alice's turn to smirk, an act that only angered her opponent.

The Witch looked ready to call forth even more powerful and terrible magic. Alice knew that she could summon another barrier for protection. Or she could take the offensive and send over her own weapons. But what good would that do? They could attack each other with magic until both were too exhausted to continue, but would they be any closer to a resolution than when they began? Destruction would only beget destruction.

She thought back to Ozma's words about unlocking the Witch's past. The how of it was still a mystery. Could one reveal the past of someone they didn't know? She had no idea what the Witch even looked like. And, in a moment of sudden clarity, the solution came to her. Perhaps Ozma's advice to remove the 'masks we wear' should be taken more literally than figuratively.

The Witch had her hands raised, moments from releasing another burst of energy. Alice offered up no defense or counter attack. Instead, she called on a different power. "Enough!" she boomed. "Nothing will come from this fighting. Don't you see that we are evenly matched now?"

The Witch replied with a disgusted scoff. "You cannot honestly believe that. You think you are an equal to me, just because you have a little magic on your side?"

From her hands, the Witch called a power wind. Holding the broom up in front of her, Alice was unmoved as the air parted to either side of her. Looking behind her, she could see that Glinda and Brax were not faring as well against it. They had been thrown from their feet and held tight against the cracks in the floor. When their fingers gave out, they would crash into the wall with such impressive speed that they would be instantly killed.

"I said enough!" She slammed the handle of the broom into the floor with a bang like a cannon. The wind immediately died, fading into nothing. Brax and Glinda were able to get back on their feet. When she was certain that they were safe, Alice returned her full attention to the Witch. "There will be no more fighting. No more destruction. And no more hiding." She blew out a breath as if extinguishing a candle.

The dark, green cloak flapped in the gentle breeze that Alice had created. The Witch made a derisive noise in response. "What is this foolishness?"

But then, as if pulled by an unseen hand, the individual threads that made up the cloak began to unravel. As the strands of fabric came apart, they floated away in the breeze until disintegrating into nothing. Slowly, the cloak eroded from existence. The Witch clutched at the loosening threads as her hood began to deteriorate as well.

[238]

When, at last, the cloak had faded from sight, Alice stood shocked. The Witch was not some hideously deformed crone, or a dangerous looking creature. She was merely a girl, a bit younger than Alice herself. Underneath, the magically flawless skin, the girl looked quite ordinary. Startled brown eyes shifted rapidly. Her light brown hair fell across her shoulders, parted into two perfectly formed braids.

Glinda stepped past Alice, confusion evident. "Dorothy?"

Chapter 21

Dorothy simply stood there for a few silent seconds. Her eyes darted from Alice to Glinda and back again, wide and alarmed. Before anyone could speak, a thick smoke filled the air, blocking Dorothy from view. When it had cleared, the space where she had stood was empty.

Alice took a small step forward. "Was that…"

"Dorothy. The Dorothy. Yes, that was her." Glinda sounded to be in complete disbelief. Her breathing came in jagged clips. "I don't understand. This makes no sense."

Brax moved to stand next to Alice, placing a hand on her shoulder. She looked up and met his eyes. "How can she be the Witch? She's supposed to be good. She was Oz's savior."

"I don't know. I just…don't know."

The great shock was having an effect on Brax, who looked as if the rug had just been pulled out from under him. His face clouded with a confused helplessness that Alice was not accustomed to. But he fought to keep himself strong

Glinda, however, had lost all sense of composure. The revelation had shaken her so badly that she could barely maintain her footing. Sinking to the floor, her body folded in on itself. Glinda, the Good Witch, was utterly broken. "This can't be. It just can't be. This has to be some kind of trick of the Witch's."

But Alice's instincts told her that it was not. She knew what she had just seen was real. The Witch had spoken with a personal contempt about the statue in the Wizard's Palace. And the statue's face had been marred beyond recognition. There was no doubt in her mind. The Witch was Dorothy Gale.

Alice wanted to ask so many question that no one would be able to answer, but a distraction came in the form of another cloud of smoke appearing out of nowhere. It was not the same smoke that Dorothy had used to escape, which had been dark and foreboding. The new cloud was of a lighter color, almost welcoming. Alice nearly cried in relief when the smoke dissipated and Scarecrow was standing there.

He rushed over to them, an urgency to his awkward steps. "Glinda, I'm glad I found you. There isn't much time."

Glinda, who was nowhere near recovered from the shock of the Witch's unmasking, looked up with vacant eyes. "What is it, Scarecrow? We have quite enough to be getting on with at the moment."

"The Council has demanded your presence back in the North. There is trouble building there."

Glinda wearily stood. She appeared to have aged years in just a few moments. A frustrated sigh escaped her mouth. "Well, we have trouble enough right here." And, regretfully, she told Scarecrow what they had discovered.

Alice had to admit that it was quite the curious sight to see a man with a cloth face display signs of shock. The fabric stretched to an unnatural length, making his features appear long and comical. Despite the gravity of the situation, she had to suppress the desire to laugh.

Scarecrow, like Glinda, was unable to process the reality in which they faced. Alice couldn't blame them. Dorothy Gale, the once savior of their world, was bringing about its destruction. Anyone would have trouble with that. Alice was having difficulty wrapping her mind around it and she didn't even know Dorothy as the others did.

"I wish there was more time for us to deal with this, but we don't have that luxury. The Council sent me to get you because the situation in Gillikin Country has reached a boiling point. The Witch's...Dorothy's...whoever she is...her forces are gathering. The flying monkeys are stationed not far from where the Council now sits. And, each minute, more and more Winkies arrive. She is preparing for a full on assault of the Council."

The news snapped Glinda back to herself. "She must have decided to attack them when she saw Alice getting close, as a contingency."

"And now that she's unmasked, she's going to be more determined to bring about an end to this." Brax busied himself by securing his axe back to his belt. "She won't be eager for us to spread around the news of her identity."

"No, she will not," Glinda agreed. "But how do we get back to the North? My magic is insufficient to make another travel sphere. We can't hope to cross the entire country in time."

But Alice thought she had a solution to that problem. "What about the shoes?" All three of them looked at her in question. "They have the power to take me home, don't they? Shouldn't they also have the power to travel across Oz instantaneously?"

Glinda looked on, thoughtfully. "No one has ever tried to use the shoes for travel within Oz's boundaries before, but the magic should work in the same manner. Right now, it is our only chance."

So all of them took hold of Alice, except for Brax who slid his hand into hers and interlocked their fingers. Once they all had a firm grasp, she pushed herself up to the balls of her feet and held her breath.

Then she tapped her heels together. One time. Two

times. And then three.

Chapter 22

Alice stood on the balcony of the large building in which the Council had taken refuge. Her second meeting with them did not go well, as tense as the first. To say the Council was not pleased with the information presented would be an understatement. Their feelings towards people from the Other Land, already low to begin with, became practically intolerant at the news that the Witch was not of Oz, not to mention being their one time heralded hero.

After hours, the Council had dismissed, once they had discussed the plans. Syrdip and Lindell had left to travel to their various people, rounding up anyone willing to fight the mounting army that they faced. The nameless Winkie representative had sequestered himself in a locked room deep in the basement so as not to succumb to the same magic that held his people prisoner and turn against his comrades. As for Cantu, she sat quietly and unmoving, not having left the meeting room.

Alice had gone to the balcony for a little fresh air after the heated meeting, but she was wishing she hadn't. In the distance, she could see the gathering hordes. There seemed to be an uncountable number of them. The crowd did not consist of only Winkies, but large beasts as well, perhaps some of the more dangerous of Oz's animal life. She could see quite a few Kalidahs amongst their ranks. And, sporadically, she spotted the outline of a large winged monkey as it flew against the night sky.

They were not ready to attack yet, that much was clear. They were still preparing, organizing themselves into whatever patterns Dorothy had ordered them into. It wasn't certain how long it would take before they were ready, but Alice was working under the assumption that it could come at any time. Alice only hoped that she would be ready for it.

Two arms snaked around her waist and she felt Brax's breath warm on the back of her neck. He pulled her close until they were pressed tightly together. "You shouldn't be out here. Staring at them is not going to ease your mind."

"My mind is going to be on them no matter where I am. At least here, I can see what I am dreading instead of just imagining it."

"Perhaps. I know it's pointless to tell you not to think about them at all. But you should try. You will need as much of your energy for when they come."

She turned herself in his arms to where she looked up

[246]

into his face. "If the Council had their say, they would force me to go home this second."

Brax shook his head vigorously. "The Council refuses to admit that they need you to get through this. They think it makes them look weak and you a threat to their power. You wield the most powerful magic in all of Oz. Whether they like it or not, you are going to be the key to bringing down the Witch... Dorothy...for good."

For some time, longer than Alice would confess, she had known that when they talked about her "bringing down" the Witch, they really meant killing her. It was the vital piece that Glinda had conveniently left out when laying out her plans. But Alice knew that was the ending everyone foresaw. She wasn't even angry about not being told. If she had, she would not have taken the news well. It was probably for the best that Glinda had let Alice come to that realization on her own. But she could not stay silent about it. "Brax, I don't know if I can kill her. I know that's what you expect of me."

He took one hand and smoothed it against her cheek, hooking her brown hair over her ear. "I don't expect anything from you, other than what you are already doing. I know that Glinda believes the only way to end this is with Dorothy's death, but that's just her anger talking. She would never be calling for the death of another living being if she hadn't been pushed to an extreme." Alice tried to look away, not comforted by his answer, but Brax's hand held her still. "But that doesn't mean it's the only option. If there is another path to take, I'm sure you will find it. I have faith in you."

She buried her face in his chest. Those were the words that she wanted to hear. They filled her with a confidence that she had been unable to build. Normally, that was never an issue for her, but the fate of an entire land was being put on her shoulders. She needed the little boost that Brax's faith could give her. Her arms tightened around him.

She pulled her head from his chest and looked at his eyes again. He was staring deeply at her. In that moment, there was no army in the distance, no upcoming battle for her to worry about. There was only his silver eyes and the night air.

"Alice, I..."

But she didn't let him finish. Instead, she leaned up and pressed her lips into his. A passionate need had filled her. A need to be even closer to him. A need to forget about what lay ahead. A need to get lost in the moment. And he obliged her.

Time passed, but not for them. It didn't matter what was happening elsewhere in the building or out on the horizon. Nothing could touch them. Dorothy, herself, could be standing on the balcony and they wouldn't have cared. Their only concern was each other and that was enough to sustain them for the time being.

But, once again, it was Glinda who brought them back to the present, by making a small, unobtrusive noise. As they pulled away from each other, slowly and with great reluctance, Alice wondered if Glinda interrupted them intentionally. It was possible the woman did not approve of what was going on between the two of them and had taken it upon herself to stop it. But then, Alice could be having a bout of paranoia. There were many things about her attraction to Brax that caused her mind to fog.

"I'm sorry that I must stop you, but Syrdip and Lindell have just returned. They have gathered a good number of citizens from the North and East to fight. If it will be enough remains to be seen." Glinda stepped farther out onto the balcony, all the way to the railing. Gone was the regal blue dress, replaced by a more form fitting shirt and pants. Her blond hair was pulled back from her face. She was dressed for battle. "They will call us for another meeting soon to strategize a battle plan."

Alice was not looking forward to meeting with the Council yet again. The last thing she needed was another round of Syrdip's harsh commentary. In the last one, even Lindell could not keep his temper in check. It would only be a matter of time before the Gillikin man came completely undone. Alice just wished that he could see past his prejudice long enough to realize that she was trying to help him and his people. What more did she have to do to prove herself to him?

"Is there any word on what Dorothy is planning?" Despite Glinda's presence, Brax refused to release Alice completely, one arm remaining around her waist. "What are we facing?"

"As near as anyone can tell, it looks like it will be a full on frontal assault. She's trying to outnumber us to a massive degree to ensure that she breaks through our defenses." Glinda placed her hands flat against the smooth railing of the balcony. She looked out on the horizon and the horde of fighters gathered there. "I'm afraid to say that it is a strategy that may work. Despite all that have come to help us, we do not have nearly her numbers."

Alice wanted, more than anything, to say something comforting to make their situation not seem so dire, something like how the power of good would always win. But that wasn't necessarily true, was it? Dorothy had once been on the side of good and look what had come of that. "What do you think happened to Dorothy?"

"I can't say." Glinda turned away from the horizon,

troubled. "I was there when she left Oz all those years ago. She enjoyed her time here, but was grateful to be going home. I could never have imagined her turning into the person she is now. It's unclear how she even got back to Oz. But this does explain why my attempts to summon her failed."

"But what could have happened to change her into a villain?"

"There's only one person who can tell us and I don't believe she is willing to give us any answers at the moment."

Alice was trying to come up with anything she could think of that would give her a clue as to what caused such a major transformation in Dorothy, any small bit of information that could give her an advantage. Before she was able to come up with anything, screams ripped through the air. What had to be every member of the assembled army off in the distance howled into the night. It was, quite simply, a battle cry.

Glinda grabbed Alice's hand. The pressure was comforting to the both of them. "Alice, despite everything that we've been through, what you may think of me, or what we've discovered on our journey, still know that I believe you are the best hope we have."

Alice nodded, taking in a deep breath. "What do we do now?"

"We prepare," Glinda's eyes hardened, "for the Ozian Civil War."

Chapter 23

Glinda had been right. The only plan Dorothy's forces had was to attack head on and attempt to overwhelm any resistance in their path. Under normal circumstances it might not have been an effective course of action, but they were far beyond normal. Syrdip and Lindell had been able to bring a large number of people to fight, but they were not soldiers. They were ordinary citizens who had been living harsh lives for a long time. They were not in any fit state to mount a defense against the Winkies and beasts under Dorothy's control.

But, despite their inadequacies, the citizens did not give up. They held back the advancing forces, keeping them from overrunning the base. Though for how long they could stop them was uncertain. Whenever one enemy fell, there were two more to take its place.

Alice watched the raging battle from the window of the highest tower. She stood there alone, Glinda and Brax leading their groups of fighters below. Her instructions were to stay there and wait for the right time to enter the fray, namely not until Dorothy showed herself. She could see them down on the ground, in the middle of a swarm of soldiers. Brax held a sword in one hand and an axe in the other. Several Winkies fell with each one of his dangerous swings. Glinda held no weapons, calling upon various enchantments to strike down her opponents. A blue mist was swirling around her which caused the enemy soldiers to fall while having no effect on the Munchkins near her.

She was told to stay out of the battle, to save her strength for when it was needed, but that was asking too much. With the broom clutched tightly in her grip, the powerful magic pumped in her veins, demanding to be used. Several times, she rained fire down on clusters of attacking Winkies before they were able to overtake Jantik. In an attempt to rescue Jellia from being eaten, she had managed to transform one of the more vicious looking Kalidahs into a creature smaller than her kitten back home, though she had no idea how she had actually done it.

As she watched, a group of eight Winkies advanced on Brax. He swung his axe with as much force as he could muster, but only two of them were dispatched. The other six had him surrounded and were beginning to overpower him. His knees buckled under their combined weight. Alice reached out the window and directed a blast towards him. All six Winkies were blown away as if struck by a bomb. It gave Brax the chance he needed to regain his balance and continue cutting his way through the enemy soldiers.

With the energy pulsing inside her, begging to be released, Alice longed to be in the middle of the battle. Considering that only a couple of hours before, nothing could have been further from the truth, it struck her as odd. Watching everyone she knew in Oz fight while she stood relatively safe in a tower didn't feel right to her. Even Scarecrow had rigged up a device to launch large chunks of debris into the crowd. So she did the only thing that she was able, used the magic to assist.

The fighting went on for an eternity. The screams from the fallen on both sides rent through the air. But it was apparent to Alice they were not on the winning side. Their lines of defense were thinning. Even as she sent more and more spells down to help, the enemy was gaining ever closer to victory.

Alice leaned out the window as far as she safely could to see. Blocking the massive front doors sat the contraption that Scarecrow was using as his weapon. A group of Gillikins were loading another large stone into the device while Scarecrow sat at the makeshift controls. Alice directed a small spell to help them lift the heavy rock.

That's when it happened. While her attention was

momentarily occupied, the winged monkeys broke through the line of soldiers blocking them. Scarecrow frantically tried to launch the stone, but he fumbled in his haste. Before Alice could react, the monkeys were on the Gillikin helpers, quickly tackling them. Even more of them pulled Scarecrow from his seat at the device. Alice tried to blast the attackers, but, in her panic, missed them, creating a hole in the ground several feet away. With nothing to stop them, the beasts pulled at Scarecrow, stretching his limbs in all directions. His body could not handle the strain and began to tear, his straw stuffing catching in the wind. His scream chilled Alice's blood. She watched as the tattered bits of fabric fell to the ground, lifeless.

She stared at what remained of her friend for several seconds before releasing her own scream into the night. Not fully conscious of her actions, she directed a massive amount of energy at the murderers. A bright streak of lightning struck. The air around the monkeys burned, engulfing their bodies in dazzling blue white flames. Any noise they made as they died was lost in the roar of the fire. She pulled back the magic and the flames died, leaving only ashes to scatter in the wind.

Alice would no longer stay in that tower, not while her friends died. Glinda be damned. She would not be confined.

With another powerful blast, the wall erupted in a hailstorm of rock, tripling the size of the window. Without so much as a second thought, Alice jumped through the hole and out of the tower. The ground and clashing throngs rushed at her at an alarming rate, but still she did not close her eyes. And, on instinct, she created a bubble around herself like she had seen Glinda do before.

She soared feet above the fight, people on both sides pausing to take notice. Dipping lower to the ground, she barreled through the crowd, knocking aside friend and foe alike. Fighters flew in the air as she surged past. She took no notice of them, searching for one face amongst them. The only person who would understand.

The bubble popped just as Alice landed in front of Glinda. The woman showed her surprise, but didn't stop her own fight against a group of Winkie soldiers. "What are you doing here, Alice? You should be in the tower." Waving her hand, Glinda caused all four of the soldiers to freeze where they stood.

"They killed him. Scarecrow." Alice could barely hear her own shout over the sound of blood pounding in her ears. "He's dead."

Pain flashed in Glinda's eyes. She stumbled, reaching out for Alice to steady herself. Her choked sob was buried in the commotion of the war waging around them. She struggled hard to regain her composure. "Not him. He was the last of her companions."

To give Glinda the moment she needed to grieve, Alice had taken over the fighting. Small bursts of energy flew from her. She didn't even need to spare a thought on where to direct them. They instantly found their targets, any Winkie or beast who had the misfortune to be near her. Each one fell with their eyes opened and a smoking wound in their chests. She didn't even glance at the fallen.

Glinda pulled in one deep breath after another, slowly coming back to herself. The pain evaporated from her eyes, replaced by a rage fiercer than any Alice had seen there before. "This will not stand." She turned back to face the warring masses. Standing there, she regarded the entire area, seeming to take in every single person. Alice saw Glinda's hands had begun to glow, at first a pale blue before changing into a bright white. Heat radiated from them.

Glinda swung her arms straight out and brought her hands together in a clap. The resulting boom shook the very air around them. The shock wave, an expanding ring of energy generated from her connected hands, passed through Alice. She had the sensation of being submerged in ice water. Others were not as fortunate. As it moved outward, the wave slammed into anyone it made contact with, picking them up and carrying them along. Person after person was caught and carried away, their yells of pain mixing together to form a collective wail. Even the small amount of grass and plants had been ripped up by their roots and tossed aside. Soon Glinda and Alice stood in the center of a large empty circle surrounded by the struggling bodies of beasts, Winkies, Munchkins, and Gillikins alike.

A figure fought to pull himself to the top of a pile of bodies. Brax struggled to get to his feet, but Alice made no move towards him. "Alice!" His yell echoed across the silent landscape, but still, she did not acknowledge him, focused only on the heavily breathing form of Glinda.

A display of that level of power must have drained Glinda of all the magic she had left to her. Alice waited for her to fall to the ground in exhaustion, but she didn't. She merely stood, looking at the clearing she had made. Even with the fighting halted, at least temporarily, anger still clouded her eyes. She looked like she was hunting for something else to strike out against.

"Now, Glinda, you really should watch your temper. You're ruining all the fun."

Dorothy floated in the air above their head without the use of broom or bubble. She made no attempt to cover her face and no one present could miss the hatred that lingered there. It was a sight that would have sent most people hiding in fear, but Alice and Glinda had their own anger to protect them.

Glinda reached back and attempted to launch a magical attack, but all she was able to produce was a few small wisps of mist that died feebly almost as soon as they were created. She was indeed drained of her power. She stared at her hands in disappointment and then up at Alice.

It wasn't the look that Glinda gave her that forced Alice into action. It wasn't even the sight of all the soldiers, hurt and beaten, surrounding her. Nor Brax limping her way. Not even the bits of Scarecrow's body scattered on the ground. It was the small, mocking laughter coming from Dorothy that made her vision turn red.

"Allow me."

Without waiting for Glinda's approval, Alice waved her hand and bolts of lightning appeared at her fingertips, streaking straight for Dorothy. They had no effect as they struck her open palm held out in Alice's direction. But Alice would not be deterred. A massive ball of light followed her initial attack. Her second attempt went much like her first. So did the third and the fourth. It only fed Alice's anger.

"I'll admit you caught me off guard when we met last, Alice. That was a very smart move, by the way. I've managed to keep my identity a secret for many years. But it changes nothing, I'm afraid. You may have managed to outsmart me once, but you will never overpower me in a fight. You must see that."

Alice had no desire to listen to Dorothy speak any longer. The sound made the blood pump faster in her ears. She sent more attacks into the air, one after another, trying to silence Dorothy. But each failed attempt only brought more taunting laughter. Magic flowed from Alice's fingers in a never ceasing current, but Dorothy managed to evade it by backing farther away and almost out of her reach.

Alice knew the fight would never end if Dorothy was allowed to continue her evasions. Soon, she would begin her own attack. While Alice wasn't particularly afraid of anything that Dorothy could throw at her, she didn't want to give her the chance. What she truly wanted was to bring Dorothy down before she had the opportunity to cause further suffering.

Then she realized that the entire time she had been fighting, the beat up old broom was in her right hand. Like the shoes, it had a magic all of its own. She had witnessed it being used back in the Wizard's Palace. It was just what she needed to even the odds against Dorothy. Instinctively, she tucked the broom between her legs and kicked off the ground.

A feeling of exhilaration washed over her as she raised

[261]

higher and higher into the air. If her mind wasn't so clouded with anger, she might have shouted with glee. The wind roared in her ears. Below her, Glinda grew smaller, but her attention wasn't on the ground. It was locked on her target.

Dorothy laughed again. "You're learning, Alice. It still won't do you any good, but at least you have the pleasure of knowing you tried." Her tone was condescending and cruel. It wasn't helping Alice keep her own temper in check. "I'll be generous and give you another opportunity. Go home, Alice. Leave Oz."

"I am not leaving, no matter what you threaten. I will not let you destroy everything. You've done enough." She spat her words at Dorothy.

"Why must you be so difficult? What is Oz to you?"

"What is it to you?" She was level with Dorothy and holding the broom steady in the air. "You saved this land once. You were a hero. They worshipped you. Why destroy it now?"

"That is my business," Dorothy snapped. "Now go back to where you came from." She floated closer to Alice, threateningly. Pointing a finger at her, she said. "There will not be another chance."

In answer, Alice released a blast of magic so powerful it rang like gunfire. Dorothy was caught off guard by the sudden explosion. At the last second, she tried to create a shield for protection, but it was too late. She was sent wheeling through the air. It took several seconds for her to right herself. When she finally did, she was a fair distance from Alice, but close enough for each to see the daggers they both shot with their eyes.

With a fierce cry, both flew through the air with alarming speed at each other.

On the ground, Glinda stood peering into the night sky. She could not make out Alice or Dorothy against the dark backdrop, but she could see the results of their fight. It looked like the kind of brilliant fireworks display that hadn't been seen in Oz since the Wizard's departure. If only it was a celebration and not the final battle that would decide the fate of her whole world.

Slowly, Brax limped to her side, his foot turned at an awkward angle. Without looking away, Glinda reached out to steady him. Together they watched events unfold. In the bright flashes, they were just able to make out figures flying away from each other and back again, like birds attacking. From so far away they could not tell one from the other. It was a guess at who was winning.

"What is she doing?" Brax asked in a hoarse whisper.

"What she was brought here to do? Saving us."

[263]

More lights blazed in the sky. Some so bright that both of them had to cover their eyes to escape their intensity. The ground shook from the concussive force of the explosions. Fissures had started to form in the dirt. The clash in the air was taking its toll on the land itself.

All around, the Ozian citizens who had been at each other's throats not long before, gathered to watch the sky. Hundreds of eyes looked on as two small specks collided over and over again. Weapons clattered to the ground, mostly forgotten with the battle having been abandoned. Both sides waited for the final outcome to see if their fight would continue or if it would finally be over.

Brax leaned even closer to Glinda. "Is there anything you can do to help her?"

She shook her head slowly. "This is her fight now."

And it was a fight that Alice had thrown herself into with everything she had. Her attacks of magic had proven to be as ineffective as Dorothy's. Both of them were just too adept at blocking the other's spells. So as an alternative, Alice used her power to craft weapons with which to fight. A blazing white axe glowed in her hand and she dove at Dorothy, who held a shield she had created. Sparks flew when the two connected and repelled each other.

"Do you know what your slaves did down there?" Alice

yelled as she let loose a shower of small daggers. "Do you even care that they murdered Scarecrow?"

Snapping her fingers, Dorothy changed the trajectory of the daggers, sending them flying straight back at Alice, who blinked them out of existence. "Scarecrow was part of Oz. Why would he be exempt from its fate?"

"He was your friend!"

A whip formed in Alice's hand. She swung the tail hard, using her magic to guide it. But Dorothy caught it and gave it a firm pull. Alice was barely able keep hold of the broom as she was dragged across the sky. With no control, she sped towards Dorothy with unnatural speed. Before she could defend herself, a hand clamped around her neck tightly. Dorothy pulled her close until their faces were inches apart.

"I have no friends in Oz." Dorothy's nails dug into the skin of Alice's throat, cutting off her air supply. Desperate fingers tried to pry the hand away, but the grip was too tight. Struggling for air, Alice's vision began to dim. "And you are a fool to think you do."

Dorothy was so intent on watching the life drain from Alice's eyes that she did not notice that the broom had fallen away. Alice swung a dangling leg upward with as much force as she could muster. Her knee made contact with Dorothy's

[265]

stomach, pushing all the air from her lungs. As the grip loosened on her throat, Alice sucked in a deep breath.

Without Dorothy holding her or the broom beneath her, Alice had nothing to keep her in the air. She started to fall from the sky. At the last second she made a grab for Dorothy's arm. Still disoriented from the blow to the stomach, Dorothy could not keep herself in the air with the added weight.

Turning over and over, each of them fought for control. The result was only a speedier fall to the ground. Dorothy clawed at Alice's face, but her fingers could not find purchase. Alice's hands had found Dorothy's throat. Using the leverage she had, Alice was able to flip one more time to where Dorothy faced the earth.

A bubble formed around both of them. Instead of using it to slow them down, Alice directed it to plummet even faster. Dorothy strained, but could not free herself. She let out a small, choked cry.

They moved faster and faster to the ground. When it seemed that there was nothing that could stop them, Alice let go of Dorothy's throat and thrust, expelling her from the bubble. Alice began to slow, but Dorothy was already speeding away. She struck the dirt with a terrifying force. A geyser of earth shot into the air and the world shook for several seconds from the impact.

Alice floated slowly to the ground, the bubble falling away when her feet touched down. She ran into the crater. Dorothy lay in the center, barely conscious. Alice stood over her, breathing heavily.

"There's a saying in Wonderland used at times like this." Raising her hand, a fiery axe appeared there. "Off with her head!"

"Alice!" Brax's voice was lost in her own scream.

The axe moved downward as if in slow motion, ready to do away with Dorothy for good. All of Oz would be saved with a single strike. The Wicked Witch would be dead.

"Alice, stop!" Ozma's voice rang in her head. "Don't let the magic control you."

The magic. It raged inside her, angered that she had stopped. It commanded her to lash out and strike against Dorothy. To kill her. It demanded revenge. It wanted her blood.

"No." The axe faded. She felt the magic fighting back, trying to force her to do its will, but she pushed it down. "There's another way."

Alice looked at Brax and Glinda, standing on the rim of the impact crater. Then she looked down at the body lying prone on the ground. Dorothy's eyes opened a fraction and met Alice's.

"Let's take you home."

Chapter 24

Three heel clicks was all it took. As Alice disappeared, she reached out with her power and pulled the three people nearest her along. They all vanished in a flash, leaving the ravaged battlefield behind, as well as the hundreds of survivors.

And in that flash, all four of them appeared again, but far from where they started. Alice stood on the exact spot she had when she first landed in Oz, deep in the heart of Munchkin Country. Barren wasteland stretched for miles in every direction, the only exception being the small wooden farmhouse tilted at an awkward angle.

Glinda rushed over. "Alice, what are you doing?"

Without looking at Glinda or Brax, she answered, "What must be done."

At Alice's feet, Dorothy had begun to fully awaken. She shook her head, clearing her daze, and pushed herself up into a sitting position. Slowly, realization dawned on her as to where she had been taken. Jumping to her feet, she turned in circles. Awe struck and horrified, she looked like she might be sick. Uncontrollable shaking wracked her body, as her eyes landed on the crumbling farmhouse.

"Why have you brought me here?" She no longer spoke with the cruel and powerful voice that Alice had heard since they met. It was not the Witch speaking, but of Dorothy Gale, a scared girl.

"This is the first place you knew in Oz, wasn't it? Your house still stands here, though I witnessed its destruction once, but now it's back. This place means something to you."

"No! It doesn't! It's just another part of this wretched land! It means nothing!"

"But it does." Glinda came forward. "In all the time you've been here, you've never come back to this place. You sent soldiers to destroy everything here. Everything except your house. They left it, untouched. And, since then, it's been hit by countless tornados, but always reforms itself in the end."

Alice took slow careful steps towards Dorothy. The girl was so distraught by her surroundings that she made no attempt to evade. Alice had to fight the magic's desire to use the opportunity to strike. "Why? Why do you keep this place?"

"As a reminder! So I would never forget all that Oz has done to me!"

"What have they done?" Alice kept her voice the complete opposite of Dorothy's. Calm and smooth as compared to angry and crazed. She had seen her father handle angry

[270]

people the same way many times. Diffusing hostile situations had been something he had excelled at. Alice was glad to have his lessons to fall back on.

"They've taken everything from me! They sent a storm to summon me, just like the first time! But their tornado ripped through my farm and destroyed everything! It killed my family! Aunt Em! Uncle Henry! Toto! Everyone I have ever loved, all gone! Because of Oz!" Dorothy turned her back on them all to face the farmhouse. Her entire body folded as her knees hit the dirt. Her shoulders heaved with unshed tears. "They stole my life. So I stole theirs."

Dorothy's pitiful state transformed Glinda. Her steel exterior melted away as she slowly moved closer. Alice could once again see the woman who protected Oz for so many years, Glinda, the Good Witch. A soft look of pity graced her face as she knelt in the dirt.

"Dorothy." Glinda reached out, but Dorothy flinched when their hands came together. "I'm so sorry for all that you lost, but we didn't summon you. We didn't attempt a Calling to the Other Land until after you began your campaign. We tried many times, but failed because you were already here."

Alice, sensing that her part was over, began to step back. Brax waited for her with open arms that took her in.

[271]

Quietly, he planted a small kiss on her cheek.

Dorothy met Glinda's eyes. "You did call me. You sent that storm."

"No, child, we didn't. You told me once that Kansas had many storms, even before you first came to Oz. The tornado that hit your farm must have been a natural one."

"No!" Dorothy pushed Glinda away from her and got to her feet. "You're lying! Oz did this to me! You did this to me!"

"But why would we? Dorothy, you were our champion, our hero. The Fall of the Wicked brought us a glorious time. We were allowed to thrive without the fear or oppression that the Witches had wrought. That would never have been possible without you." Glinda held her arm wide, pleadingly. "We thought we were giving you a gift, the only one we could, by leaving you to your life in Kansas. I would never have called you for anything less than the Witch."

Dorothy stood, frozen, as if she had been punched in the stomach. She was having trouble forming words. Reality was beginning to take a hold of her. "But..."

"It is the truth. We would never have done such a thing, not after everything you did for us."

A powerful shudder ran through Dorothy. "What have I done?"

From nowhere, a mighty wind began to howl. Brax

[272]

tensed, but Alice put a calming hand on his arm. "Wait. Let it come."

With an extraordinary swiftness, the sky above them began to churn. Spinning, the clouds formed a funnel that lunged for the ground. The tornado, larger and stronger than the one they had seen strike the house before, landed near them. Alice sent magic to anchor their feet, even Dorothy's, so as not to be swept up by the immense wind.

The twister moved, cutting a path in the earth beneath it. With a resounding thunder, it slammed into the farmhouse, shredding it board by board. In seconds, no trace of it remained to prove it had ever been there in the first place. It's mission complete, the tornado retreated back into the sky.

Dorothy watched the destruction of her house in pain. Her whole body quivered, vibrating like a tuning fork. Once the tears started, they came in earnest. She wrapped herself in a tight embrace. "No." She whispered the word over and over again until it was buried in her sobs. And then she released a scream so terrible that it gripped at Alice's heart. The air picked it up and joined in.

In every direction, Oz itself wailed in agony.

Alice was inundated with the pain of the land and her legs could no longer support her. Brax held on tightly, lowering her to the ground. Tears sprang to her eyes as terrible anguish flooded her body. The suffering of Oz had become hers, amplified by its magic. It took everything to maintain consciousness, but she had to. She had to witness.

And still Dorothy screamed, louder and more horrible than anything that came before it. It built upon itself, past the point of deafening, and continued to rise. Her head gave an impressive jerk, pointing her face to the sky. And with that, magic erupted from Dorothy and rushed, like a river, until it reached the clouds. It went on forever, a seemingly never ending stream of light pouring itself back into Oz.

Then, with a concussive force that threw everyone from their feet, the magic exploded. The resulting shockwave expanded outward, covering the world in a blinding white light.

***

Across the land, life came back to Oz.

In Gillikin Country, the citizens who had gathered to fight, fell to their knees and wept as the ground at their feet began to sprout lush green grass for the first time in anyone's memory. The Winkies grabbed one another in tight embraces as the magic that had bound them for so long lifted, getting their first taste of freedom in years. And bits of straw rolled across

[274]

the ground to stuff itself into the cloth of the rapidly mending body of Scarecrow.

In Western Oz, inside the Witch's former castle, scraps of tin gathered themselves and fused together in the shape of a man. As the last piece fell into place, Nick Chopper opened his eyes and took in a deep breath.

In Quadling Country, the floods that had overrun the entire section of the country receded, revealing the land beneath it. The water ran all the way down, past the southern border, where it transformed back into a sandy desert with a sparkling crystal castle overlooking it. The echo of a great lion's roar sounded in the air.

In the Emerald City, buildings repaired themselves, returning the former glory of the metropolis. Holes in the Wizard's Palace filled with debris from the streets. On the highest floor of the highest tower, the scars left on the golden statue disappeared, revealing the smiling face that had been carved so long ago.

And in Munchkin Country, yellow bricks flew through the air and laid out the shape of a road. Flowers as large as people pushed up from the green grass. Small houses came into existence as if grown from seeds. Birds took flight from trees as they climbed from the soil. The clouds dashed across the sky as if caught in an incredible wind, until they disappeared from sight, leaving behind a brilliant blanket of blue and a warm yellow sun.

At the base of the newly formed road, Alice and Brax were climbing to their feet. Glinda already stood, as much transformed as everything else. No longer did she wear the pants and blouse. Her majestic blue gown glittered in the sunlight. In her hand, she held a long, thin scepter topped with the crystal relic. Tears ran past her wide smile.

Dorothy lay on her stomach, arms and legs splayed out. The Witch's black garb had vanished, replaced with a blue and white checked dress and small black shoes. At a glance, one would never have assumed it was the same person that had caused Oz so much trouble. She looked like a girl, a young one, fresh with innocence.

She slowly began to stir. Glinda was there to help her to her feet. "Dorothy? Child, are you alright?"

Dorothy could not give her an answer. She was still in so much pain, but there was no anger left in her. She fell into Glinda, who was only too happy to envelope the girl in her arms.

"You'll be fine now, Dorothy. Let us take care of you."

Alice and Brax stood apart. Instinctively, they found their way into each other's arms. "It's so beautiful." Alice marveled at the beauty all around her. The colors. The smells. The warmth. At last, Oz the way it was meant to be.

"It is beautiful once more. Thanks to you." And Brax leaned down and kissed her in the warm sunlight.

Chapter 25

The people of Oz celebrated for a week. Parades. Dinners. Parties. And, of course, Alice had to be present at all of them. Everyone had to give their thanks, shake her hand, kiss her cheek. Construction was already underway for her statue that would stand in the Wizard's Palace, next to Dorothy's. Alice was honored to be there, more for the people than for herself. She did not need to be thanked for saving them, but they needed to do the thanking.

Dorothy was invited to all of the celebrations as well, but attended few of them. People were unsure of how to act in her presence at the ones she did. Most were forgiving, hugging her and weeping with her over her losses. Others were not, giving her sidelong glances and stepping quickly away. For her part, Dorothy accepted the condolences and the scorn equally, taking the punishment for her numerous crimes. When she was not needed, she spent all of her time locked in her rooms at the palace.

But an end to the celebrations had to come, and Alice had to face the fact that she needed to return home. Days before, she would have been eager to leave, but once the time had arrived, she found herself taking pause. She had managed to push thoughts of what was to come aside for almost a week.

When she wasn't busy with the people's adulation, she gave every free moment to Brax. He had showed her the Emerald City, the way it was supposed to be seen. And they had found as much time as they could to be alone, anywhere they could manage it. Their kisses were like air, they couldn't get enough. At the final celebration, they disappeared for some time to the Wizard's throne room. And Glinda was not there to interrupt them.

But those times were over. The people had to get back to their lives, or to try to create new ones now that they had the option. Oz had to get back to the business of living. And Alice had to get back to her family, who were probably sick with worry.

Glinda, Brax, Dorothy, Scarecrow, and Alice gathered in the throne room. Syrdip had insisted that he, and the rest of the Council, be present at Alice's departure, but Glinda quickly denied him. He went on for quite some time about how Glinda did not have the authority to deny him anything, to which she waved her hand and transported him to a field in the northernmost area of Oz. "That man will never learn, will he?" Glinda and Alice had shared a laugh over it.

[279]

Scarecrow was the first to step forward. "I have so much to thank you for. Much more than I could ever repay."

Alice hugged him, squeezing his soft body tightly. "You standing here is all the thanks I need. You have no need to repay anything."

Pulling away, Alice moved to the next person, wiping a few stray tears. The longer her goodbyes took the more chance she would not be able to keep her composure. Dorothy stood next in line, shifting uncomfortably, unsure as to whether she should even be there. Alice pulled her close.

"Are you sure you won't come back with me?"

Dorothy shook her head. "I'm not ready for that yet. I need more time. Besides, I have to make amends where I can here. It is the least I owe them."

Looking Dorothy in the eye, she said, "When you are ready, I will be there. Perhaps I can even visit Kansas."

Dorothy simply nodded.

And then it was Glinda's turn. The woman beamed at Alice as they grasped hands. "Oh Alice, you've done so much more than I could have hoped. When you fell at my feet, I never imagined that you would be able to accomplish this marvel. We may have had our moments, but you never abandoned us. I will forever be in your debt." Glinda wiped tears out of her eyes. She had been crying tears of joy a great deal over the course of the week. "I will never forget you."

Despite everything that had happened between them, Alice would also miss Glinda. Her experience with magic, and almost losing control, had taught her a deeper understanding of the woman. She knew how anger could take over, making one act drastically for "the good". She pulled Glinda into a deep hug. "I'll never forget you either. I would not have been able to do any of this if you hadn't pushed me every step of the way, no matter what your reasons might have been." The two shared a smile before letting go.

The moment that she most dreaded had finally arrived. Brax stood next in line, a completely different person. Dressed in fine clothes without an arsenal at his side, he made an even more dashing figure. He looked down at the floor, unable to meet her eyes. Reaching a hand under his chin, she lifted his head up. She could never have pictured his eyes wet with tears.

"What will you do now?" She hadn't needed to whisper, for Glinda had ushered the others to the other side of the room so they might have a chance at a private farewell.

"I don't know. Now that the land is restored I can do anything I choose. I might go back to my father's farm and start it up again. It's only right that it should be part of this new Oz."

Alice got a mental image of Brax working the farm,

carrying on his father's work. The picture made her smile, imagining that would please him. More than anything, she wanted to know that Brax would have a good life after she was gone, to know that he was happy. "I wish you could come with me."

His hand moved to her hair, a gesture she had grown to love. "I wish I could too, but I can't. This is my world. Now that it has been set right, my place is here. Just like your place is back in the Other Land, no matter how much I want you to stay."

"I don't want to say goodbye, Brax."

He looked down at her with a sad smile. "Then don't. It will never be goodbye. We may still see each other one day."

She didn't believe that, and she knew he didn't either. They were seeing each other for the final time. She stopped trying to keep them at bay and let her tears come. Brax wiped them away with his thumb, leaving her cheek wet. "I'll see you then."

Their lips met, pressing against each other in urgent need. She tried to take so much from the kiss. The feel of him. The taste of him. The smell of him. Anything she could hold on to and remember long after she was gone. When at last they parted, it was with a sense of finality that made her stomach twist into a knot.

"I have to go now." It broke her heart to say the words,

but if she stayed any longer, she would never leave. She took a couple of steps away from him, forcing herself not to run back into his arms. Her tears made him a blurry image. She wiped them clear, needing to see him until the very end.

Raising to her toes, she choked back a sob. Each heel click was like a cannon in her ear. One. Two. Three.

And the world was gone.

Epilogue

The soles of Geraldine Gulch's shoes echoed against the linoleum floor of the long term care ward. Even though it was almost noon, the hallway was quiet. It was always quiet. The patients made little noise and most visitors came only on the weekends. It made Geraldine's rounds go by a lot quicker when she didn't have family members' constant questions to slow her down, which meant she was able to spend time with her more colorful patients, like Mr. Johnson, who told the funniest stories about his family, or Ms. Buchannon, who loved to go on and on about her many suitors.

And then there was her favorite, the girl in the last room on the right. Dorothy Gale had been a patient in the hospital longer than Geraldine had worked there. She had actually met the girl once, many years ago. She had been out visiting her sister, a neighbor of the Gale farm. Her sister had been a miserable woman, going on and on, detailing what a pain the girl was, but Geraldine had never found that to be true. Dorothy had seemed like such a sweet child. And the stories she used to tell always made Geraldine smile.

It was horrible what happened to her and her family. Sadly, it was a story that she had heard many times over the years. In Kansas, tornados came, did their damage, and left. Geraldine had been through three and lived to tell about it. Dorothy was different though.

She had been through the notes written on Dorothy's case since she was first brought to the hospital. Doctor after doctor had seen her, but none could find anything physically wrong with the girl. She had suffered a great trauma from the tornado and the death of her family, but had no injuries herself. All the same, she lay in a coma, asleep to the world, for years.

Geraldine silently thought that maybe it was for the best that Dorothy slept, knowing what she would awaken to.

Pushing open the door to Dorothy's room, Geraldine let out a gasp and nearly dropped her clipboard. The old woman next to Dorothy's bed showed no sign of surprise, just continued to sit with her hands in her lap. Geraldine was confused. In all the years, no one had ever visited Dorothy. There was no one left to visit her.

"I'm sorry, ma'am. I wasn't expecting to find anyone in here."

"Then it should really be me apologizing, shouldn't it?"

[285]

The woman wasn't from Kansas. She had an English accent and that would definitely be commented on. Turning in her chair, the woman smiled. "I'm Alice. Alice Hargreaves."

Still confused, and a bit protective, Geraldine stepped farther into the room. "I'm sorry, but do you know Dorothy?"

"Oh yes, we're quite old friends. We knew each other back from our days in Oz. I've just come to sit with her for a while."

Oz. That was the funny name of the place in all of Dorothy's old stories. Geraldine gave her a questioning look. But she was satisfied that the old woman, Alice, must have been acquainted with Dorothy in some way. How else would she have known such a ridiculously made up name? "Well, I'll just leave you to it."

"Thank you," Alice said as the nurse backed out of the room, leaving her alone with Dorothy.

Alice enjoyed a small smile at the nurse's expense. It had become a sort of personal joke to her over time. Every once in a while, she would drop the name Oz, just to see the odd looks it raised. It was one of the small joys that she had created for herself.

It had taken her a long time to track the girl down. Given that she had very little to go on, that wasn't much of a surprise. Kansas was a big place, but it finally happened. A friend from home, who was traveling in the States, had made some inquiries on her behalf and discovered that Dorothy was a patient in the hospital. She held on to that information for almost a year, trying to create an excuse to visit that would not make her sound insane. With Reginald gone, it shouldn't have been so difficult, but with lots of family comes lots of questions.

But an excuse had finally presented itself. Columbia University had invited her to a celebration of the centennial of Lewis Carroll's birth. She did not want to attend. The last thing she thought the world needed was to celebrate anything having to do with that dreadful Mr. Dodgson or his book, but it gave her the excuse she sought. So, after spending the briefest amount of time pretending to be Alice in Wonderland again, she made her exit and caught a train to Topeka. Arriving earlier that morning, she went straight to the hospital.

Seeing Dorothy sleeping in that bed caused a flood of memories to wash over her. Glinda. Scarecrow. Jellia. And, most of all, Brax. Over the years, and there had been many of them, she had thought about Brax often and wondered how his life turned out. Did he settle down with someone? Did he have children? Did he have a good life?

In all her life, she had never recaptured the same feelings she had shared with Brax, not with Leopold or even

[287]

Reginald. Yes, she loved them, but not how she had loved Brax. That was something reserved for her memory. She refused to share that with anyone, not even when it came to naming her children. Brax was hers and hers alone, a secret she had kept for the majority of her life.

In her bed, Dorothy began to stir. Each movement produced a small groan. The voice was rasping and weak, distorted with neglect. The sheets rustled as her limbs came to life.

Alice leaned closer, breathless. "Dorothy?" She placed a hand on Dorothy's shoulder. If she was lucky, the girl would wake up before the nurse was alerted. It would not do to be interrupted.

The eyes that she hadn't seen in sixty years blinked open.

Dorothy strained to turn her head. The old woman looked so different than the girl from Oz. The face was weathered and aged, but it was the same person. Finding the strength, she moved her hand into Alice's.

"He...he's happy."

Tears came to both of their eyes. Alice lifted Dorothy's hand and gave it a kiss. "Welcome home, Dorothy."

www.ingramcontent.com/pod-product-compliance
Lightning Source LLC
Chambersburg PA
CBHW020258200626
46816CB00001BA/349